THE PALE
ONES

Biography

BARTHOLOMEW RICHARD EMENIKE BENNETT was born in Leicester, the middle son of an American father and English mother. He has studied and worked in the US and New Zealand, and has a First Class Honours degree in Literature from the University of East Anglia. Since graduation he has had various jobs: primarily software developer, but also tutor, nanny, data-entry clerk and call-centre rep, project manager and J-Badger (ask your dad), painter and decorator, and (very slightly) handy-man, working at locations all across the United Kingdom. He has also been known to dabble in online bookselling.

The Pale Ones is his first published work, although he has been writing fiction continuously, long-form and short, since 2002. Currently he is at work on a novel about three children who experience a long, wintry December filled with gifts. Of the unusual variety. And trials. Of the trying variety.

Currently he lives in southeast London, with his wife and two young children. He is a longstanding member of *Leather Lane Writers Group*, and since childhood, a dedicated reader of all manner of books, but especially tales of the "horror". And in fact, some of the paper-packed rooms that feature in The Pale Ones bear a remarkable resemblance to locales in his own abode...

Praise for Bartholomew Bennett

"An insidiously disquieting tale, flavourfully told. What begins as a dark comedy of book collecting gradually accumulates a profound sense of occult dread, which lingers long after the book is finished. It's a real addition to the literature of the uncanny and an impressive debut for its uncompromising author."
RAMSEY CAMPBELL,
author of the *Brichester Mythos trilogy*

"To a soundtrack of wasps, The Pale Ones unsettles in the way of a parable by some contemporary, edgeland Lovecraft, or another of the authors the used-book dealers in this story no doubt seek out, Arthur Machen. The unnerving images which flicker in a sagging English landscape of charity shops, seaside bed and breakfasts and amusement arcades, washed with stale beer, linger in my imagination ages after reading."
ANTHONY CARTWRIGHT,
author of *Heartland, BBC Radio 4 Book at Bedtime*

THE PALE ONES

Bartholomew Bennett

nkandescent

Inkandescent

Published by Inkandescent, 2018

Text Copyright © 2018 Bartholomew Bennett

Printed and bound in Great Britain by Clays Ltd, Elcograf S.p.A.

MIX
Paper from
responsible sources
FSC® C018072

ISBN 978-0-9955346-8-1 (paperback)
ISBN 978-0-9955346-9-8 (Kindle ebook)

1 3 5 7 9 10 8 6 4 2

www.inkandescent.co.uk

To the memory of Anne and Tina

Writer's Note

About ten or fifteen years ago, it was entirely possible to make quick, easy money selling second-hand books through various online marketplaces – the best known being eBay and Amazon (although there were, and continue to be, other alternatives also). In the intervening ten years, the used book market online has changed substantially – commission rates have increased, postage charges have more than doubled, and changes to search algorithms and methods have in some instances narrowed the demand for certain, once-profitable older editions. And all the while, a tendency towards oversupply has steadily suppressed prices. Selling books thus is still absolutely a possibility, but the barriers to entry for the novice are much higher.

1

The second time I met Harris, he was rustling around the bookshelves of my local hospice shop. Whilst working my way along the parade of worn titles, I became aware of a greasy little smoke-like presence, a figure more dark wool overcoat than actual person, riffling through one of the boxes of sheet music in a brisk, cursory fashion suggestive of scant interest in the contents. I couldn't pretend I wasn't annoyed. The shop, cavern-like if not cavernous, was not ever busy and I was used to having the books, in their haphazard stacks and misaligned rows, to myself. The overcoat's extreme proximity, and the way it backed into me without revealing its owner's face, bordered on the uncomfortable, if not outright rude. I took a grudging sideways step, attempting to refocus on the grubby shelving and the broken, battered spines thereon. But some subliminal cue convinced me that I was being observed and so, annoyed by the sense of covetous eyes on the growing hoard of paperbacks in the crook of my arm, I made the error of taking a further – this time unguarded – glance at him.

And mistake indeed it proved to be.

I had read his body, or at the very least his posture, all wrong. He was facing me, poised and ready to seize his opportunity. It might have been a smile – or perhaps something else, small and dark and malicious – that rustled through the hair around his mouth.

— It's that one you want, he said. — Nice little seller. Best unit you'll find in this place. Best you'll find along the high street.

He eased the hardback from the shelf. The tatty dust-jacket, its edges nicked and torn, bore the title in an archaic, angular font: *World War II Destroyers*. Below that the surname of the author, Jacobs, was just legible, its once-red lettering faded away to prosthesis pink.

— Fifty or sixty for that, maybe as much as seven-five if the wrapper there was in better shape. And after what they'll ask for it in here...

He whistled quietly, and there again went the agile little rodent through his beard. From his hand movement I understood that by wrapper, he meant the dust jacket. He had an air of expertise; everything about him was persuasive, high-quality antique – from the dirty grey of his peppery, oiled hair to the papery, sun-worn skin around his eyes. His clothing conjured a distant suggestion of armour or carapace: wool and leather and silk, all top-end, perhaps even hand-tailored, and all lightly soiled. And his smell: a tight, high blend of cold, dead tobacco, mixed with something like turpentine, and old, desiccated sweat.

— I'd take it myself, but I've done all right this morning already. Got a vanload of academic texts from a house clearance job parked just up the hill: Routledge, Verso, OUP. All tight and tidy... I like to help the younger generation; lambs haven't much chance. Not the way it's all going, hand-cart-wise...

I was unsure whether by 'younger generation' Harris was referring to me as an admittedly rather novice book dealer, or to the students upon whom he intended to unleash his stock of dog-eared academic disquisitions. But his having sized me up so assiduously felt something of an embarrassment: I imagined myself inconspicuous, the nature of my business in the shop opaque – simply a customer, perhaps a keen reader. In truth, the books I was searching out were units to be bought and sold; the internet had, at least for a while when all of this happened, made doing so a viable money-making operation.

— Go on, lad, Harris urged. — Someone'll snap it up within the month. I gah-ran-*tee* it. For the plates alone, if nothing else... Take the blessed thing.

I didn't want to; the shabbiness of the book didn't appeal to me any more than did the odd little man pushing it forward. But I wasn't gathering for my personal collection. And if I was making just a fifth of the profit he promised on every book I sold, well...

— There'll be something another time you can do for me, he said.

For some reason, I found that reassuring. Perhaps because it felt familiar – something I'd heard before, or a deal I'd already struck. As I reached for the book though, I noticed with a twinge of revulsion that his middle finger had wrapped around it an old fabric plaster, its pinkness transmuted to the dirty grey of a putty rubber used to stipple charcoal. I thought that I could just make out the horrible green-brown of some ulcerated wound visible underneath the sticky, curled edge. I found it in myself to thank him for his advice, and turned back to my perusal of the shelves.

He refrained, thankfully, from offering any further tips, and after examining a few of the ancient browning pamphlets clogging up shelf space, wandered off to rummage through an immense wicker hamper crammed full of the shop's perennial overstock of VHS cassettes – they had on a multibuy offer of the deviously illogical sort only ever seen in charity shops: twenty-five pence each, or twelve for a pound. Finally, before heading to the counter, I tucked the Destroyers book back onto the shelf. I'd spotted an unpleasant looking brownish stain along the bottom edge, and had decided it simply wasn't worth the hassle.

Despite that, Harris had certainly been right about the asking prices: the shop was run on behalf of a local hospice, and was in a still grotty enough area of south London that they let their stock go for pennies. Hardbacks might command as much as a pound; that was if you could stop the old dears running the till from further discounting your purchase. They seemed absurdly grateful that you'd freed up more space for them to jam in a selection of their usual fodder: forgotten bestsellers, superseded study aids and newspaper giveaways. But for every fifty – perhaps even one hundred – items of dross there would be one book with actual resale value.

There was a hold-up while the customer before me, a stooped, elderly looking gent, the helix of his left ear partially eaten away by a sore the colour of a waterlogged raisin, tried unsuccessfully to negotiate an enlargement of the value of the sticky-looking fifty pence piece he proffered up in payment. Finally rebuffed, the man traipsed away, his intended purchase, a pathetically out-of-season snowglobe, left abandoned on the counter glass.

— Some people, blurted one of the women behind the till, no doubt intending the declaration to be overheard. — Do they not understand that we're operating on behalf of charity?

She squinted distrustfully at me. — You *get* it, don't you, young sir?

I gave her my best smile and nodded.

— Yes, she said, looking far from convinced. — I can see you do.

As it happened, I was used to a certain amount of dissimulation. I felt obliged always to grin and reassure the staffers that of course I'd enjoy my reading.

— It's two-for-one on books, the second lady told me, after

totting up the numbers. — You're on an odd here. Did you want to find another?

Although this particular shop frequently did sell off their stock cheap, I hadn't noticed any of the usual handwritten signs. And I knew this particular helper wasn't one of the keener edges there. I paused, momentarily uncertain. Harris's pick waited skewiff, spine reversed, along the top of a row of Mills & Boon.

— You might as well, said the first assistant.

She meant, I judged, quite the opposite. And that, for me, settled it.

The tactic, as far as I could tell, was to pair the borderline senile with the partially-sighted, in the vague and generally unfulfilled hope that each would compensate for the other's inadequacy, rather than multiply one another's errors. That day they managed a modest accuracy: despite having convinced me to take away more of their stock, they still contrived to undercharge me by a pound or so. To compound my sense of guilt, I noticed as they tallied up that they'd miscounted originally – I'd had twelve in the first place. With the scant time remaining to them on the earthly plane, it seemed unfair to ask for the waste of a further fortnight in rerunning their glacial calculation. I'd seen enough of the more belligerent of the two to know she'd take offence at my correcting their joint reckonings, so instead I merely stuffed my change into their desktop collection jar.

The simpler of the two volunteers smiled at me.

— Bless you.

The other peered with something like revulsion at the blue plastic chalice, as though I'd seen fit to defecate into the Holy Grail itself.

— Another one, I heard her say as I made my way to the

door, her late December voice breeding resignedness with dis-approval.

The other volunteer tried to shush her. It served only to put an edge on her counterpart's tongue:

— Oh yes. A knight, that one. A regular Roland.

I paid her little mind, busily wagering myself that the copy of Drummond and Manning's *Bad Wisdom* (the Penguin edi-tion, a cultish favourite, bore a gilt spine and cover, as if in happy recognition of its worth as a used book) that I'd found would trump Harris's tip, both in terms of price and speed of sale. Some low, unbridled part of me thrilled to the thought of comparing dividends.

Outside, I decided that I'd done more than enough to have earned my mid-morning coffee and so eased a couple doors up to a newly-opened coffee shop – its pre-distressed furnishing and outrageous prices at that time something of a departure for the area.

It was as I stood waiting to order that Harris materialised at my shoulder. I'd taken the book I was reading out of my bag in anticipation of having to dump everything else I was carrying at the counter: a gathering of blinking, squinty-eyed new mothers, their accompanying infants in strollers, had dammed up access to the few remaining free tables.

— Surely you're not going to refuse me a cup of black? Not after the wedge I just slipped into your trouser pocket.

I motioned at the chalkboard menu.

— Whatever you want.

— Or...

He left that hanging there long enough that I felt obliged to look over at him with expectant eyebrows.

— ... you could just give me that Lowry there.

Under the Volcano was the book I had in hand. A ten-year-old Picador reprinting worth, I was quite certain, absolutely nothing. My attempt to read it had stalled early in the New Year, around the time Karen left for Japan. Reading about a hopeless drunk hadn't seemed like much of a transport then. But I didn't ever like to give up on a book, and I'd retrieved it just that morning from the bottom of my bedside stack, my initial foray still bookmarked about a fifth of the way in. I hesitated, primarily because I'd have to find something else to read while I drank my coffee. But then, quite reflexively, I opened the book. The object marking my place was a strip of old-school passport photos: Karen and I stuffed together into the booth, gurns growing more grotesque with each shot.

— Sorry, I told Harris, — I need to keep hold of this.

I knew there was a streak of irrationality to my decision – it would be trivial enough to find another copy of the book. But somehow letting it go would have felt too much of a betrayal. He looked disgruntled at my refusal, his eyes still fixed on the photographs.

Harris made some dismissive, not wholly cogent comment then about broken spines and the disappointment of imperfection. I glanced down, annoyed. I took great care always not to crease bindings. I treasured all my books. Even the beach reads.

— But it's perfect, I told him.

— Of course it is, he said, his voice low and mean. — Everything's just perfect.

I tucked the book away under my arm. But Harris hadn't finished.

— I *could* force your hand, you know.

I didn't know what that meant – what the *hell* that meant. But it wouldn't do, losing my temper. I wasn't, I reminded myself, to do that any more. I'd made a decision – and it held, whatever the reason for my anger. He was waiting, his face expectant, and I felt a sudden, lucid conviction that he *knew* already the suggestion I was ready to make: that he might mount the tailpipe of his book-loaded van.

— How about that coffee? I asked instead, not quite able to inject the right amount of goodwill into my offer.

— No, no. He smiled. — Got to go and make money.

And then, clapping me on the shoulder hard enough to spill the drink I had just lifted from the counter, he was away again. It was funny because Harris had appeared initially, I was quite certain, at my right, meaning he had to have somehow ghosted his way out of the seating area and through the crowd of mothers. But I had been sure that he had still been in the hospice shop when I left, sizing up their selection of flat caps. Glancing out into the morning sunlight I caught sight of him across the road, slipping through the gauntlet of broken, dowdy smokers clustered about the even dowdier entrance to the Railway Tavern.

He wouldn't be making any money in there I thought – rather archly – to myself. But then I noticed he had stopped to speak with one of the men outside: a stoop-shouldered gentleman, familiar in his frailty.

Harris lifted something from his pocket.

Sunshine winked from a clear sphere: the ornamental snowglobe. Harris pressed it into the man's hand before disappearing into the gloom.

2

The dream I had after that encounter was a simple one.

There was a circular ashtray, its rim covered with a great fan of long white cigarettes. I pulled the cigarette that belonged to me to my lips, where I discovered that it wasn't a cigarette at all but the bone, denuded of all flesh, of my middle finger. I drew on it nonetheless – through my thumb, as though that digit were somehow a pipe stem, as in the logic of dreams. It was then I discovered – wrong again! – that the bone of my finger was not bone but a roll of hollow, empty paper, quickly consumed by the red smouldering ring of the lit tip.

Without alarm, I tried simply to knock the ash from the paper-bone of my finger. But there was no space in the ashtray.

Only then did the pain arrive in my finger.

I woke breathless, craving for the first time in years (I'd given up for Karen – or perhaps she had lent me the strength to give up for myself) a cigarette.

3

Harris had been half-right. Jacob's *Destroyers* did indeed command a high price – higher even than he'd suggested. Book-Finder.com had listings for only a few copies, most of which were the same sellers offering the same book for slightly varying prices across the usual sites. Its sales ranking on Amazon, though – not infallible, but a good indicator – was risible. I listed my stained copy and promptly forgot about it. *Bad Wisdom*, on the other hand, sold for a sum in the mid-twenties that same week, justifying my confidence. Yet if it took a year – even two – to sell Harris's tip, it would still be a tidy piece of business.

In fact I paid neither book any great mind. With the arrival of summer, order numbers had greatly increased and I was running low on high-value stock. The tiny boxroom – nominally a study – in my mean, little ex-local-authority flat was filled with books, CDs and decrepit but rare video cassettes (mostly deleted titles, or films still unavailable on DVD). What twelve months before had been a modest sideline (searching out my various fictional enthusiasms, mostly unfashionable twentieth-century American stuff: Barth and Coover and Gaddis, the then-out-of-print Shirley Jacksons, selling the odd found gem to fund some of the harder-to-find titles) had expanded to become my most reliable income source.

Yet the nature of the enterprise meant that, on the whole, the good stuff sold fast while the useless sat gathering dust. And lemons, on my shelves, were starting to outnumber hotcakes by some margin. Relatively recent – and certainly post-

60s books – with ISBNs were easy. You could check their going rate pretty much on the spot; all that was needed was a smartphone. It was the older books, the rare and the antiquarian, that were a little beyond that scope. Their market was subtly different: the rewards were bigger but trickier to cash in on, the information available less perfect, buyers less likely to purchase unseen. Even with the newer books, the information from Amazon and the like wasn't faultless. A high asking price didn't necessarily convert to a high selling price if no one wanted the book in the first place, and the sales rankings weren't as transparent as they might at first seem.

I'd long since lost whatever appetite I'd had for the contracting – coding projects and bug fixes – that had been my previous income source. Karen's ten and twelve hour days at a job for which she only very occasionally expressed any kind of enthusiasm, had long since become – to my mind, at least – a form of undiagnosed insanity. I'd already frittered away my twenties, plus a little small change, on work I didn't care about, in and amongst the usual phonies and users and flat-out liars. I didn't care to lose any more time.

The truth of the matter was that without Karen there, I had let things slip. Even before I'd started to accumulate books, we'd had barely enough space for our personal things: the shoes piled in corners, the mismatched furniture, the exercise equipment – Swiss ball, yoga mat, mountain bike – that had turned the hall into a slalom course. I had discussed endlessly with Karen the possibility of expanding my stock to levels whereby I might derive from it an income reliable enough to hire a storage lock-up. Really, I could have afforded as much already. But there was still something amateurish, and thus pleasurable, about my enthusiasm for the business; I liked to keep the books close. They kept me safe, insulated the walls.

And I never felt as though I had enough.

Given that, it was unsurprising that I should fall for Harris's offer when it came.

He showed up in the Bricklayer's three weeks or so after our meeting in the hospice shop. It was late; I'd been watching a game – a World Cup qualifier, I seem to remember – with a friend, who after a quick noseful of Harris, had made his excuses – a dawn phone meeting with Mumbai colleagues or some such vitality-draining horseshit. I, on the other hand, had no pressing plans for the morning, and accepted the offer of a pint. As it turned out, Harris was already somewhat wobbly – in terms of common sense, at least. When his beautifully worded assessment of the relationship between nylon replica shirts and bedroom onanism attracted a little too much of the wrong sort of attention, I'd felt obliged to help the old fellow out. Prior to that he'd been talking books – and money – and I wanted to hear more about both.

— Bit bloody useful, aren't you, son? he said, as I hauled him off outside.

I didn't respond to the comment, but he wouldn't let it go:

— Been in the services? he pressed. — You looked bloody dangerous just now.

I had looked nothing of the sort. If anything I had looked big – big enough to move him – and drunk enough for the less humourless of the footie fans to think twice. Then again, we might just have been lucky.

— You don't need any special training, I told him, — to know when to leave off a bunch of angry, pissed-up losers.

— Two minutes more and they'd have been buying our beer.

Harris's voice was gleeful.

I sighed. — Someone would have been paying for some-*thing*, anyway.

— You've got an officer's voice, he said. — And those cold, quiet eyes. Send the fodder out to their fate, he snapped his fingers — *just* like that.

He grinned then, and I didn't know whether he was taking the piss; despite his ragbag range of accents, he tended eventually to lapse back into the sort of concise, uninflected speech that suggested a cheque-book education.

— Smile, and smile, and be a villain.

I only muttered the words, but Harris was close enough to hear. And far too suave to let confusion show on his face.

I wasn't altogether sure of the provenance of the quote. It had the air of Shakespeare, but for some reason, I couldn't shake the idea that it came from Goethe. I'd have to look it up to be absolutely sure. Regrettable, but that was the way my mind worked: precision tempered by the merest fraction of uncertainty.

Up at my flat, it didn't take long to shift the conversation back towards sources of stock. At the time, I think I actually imagined that I was playing Harris. He chatted away happily in generalities, contriving to reveal no specifics whatsoever. So I pushed a little; I pushed on him also a glass or two of a horrible blended scotch that seemed to have been haunting my kitchen cupboard forever. Eventually, he told me that if I was really interested then he'd take me along on his next out-of-towner:

— Friday week, stopover somewhere up in Yorkie. My van. You drive. You load. You keep an even quarter of whatever we get – at cost, mind. Be about five–six hundred books – all saleable.

— Oh yeah – and all profitable? I asked.

— Oh, more than, said Harris. As if unsatisfied, he amplified the comment: — More than…

What I really wanted was to learn more about the possibility of acquiring books en masse. Picking up stock piecemeal – book by book in the thrift shops – meant that although I only purchased copies that I thought I could sell, those books were relatively expensive – and the work was time consuming. Yet the deal Harris offered wasn't fantastic – it would only be worthwhile if I gained an understanding of his methods, perhaps making a useful contact or two along the way. Then also, there was his expertise in the rare and antiquarian: might I also acquire some of that knowledge? I wasn't entirely certain that his apparent learnedness wasn't a pose, or con.

— I'll guarantee you first pick, he said.

And that promise sealed it – or, rather, the drunken, munificent smirk that accompanied the pledge. I couldn't, apparently, tell muck from gold. Either that or Harris had some other plan for skimming off the cream. But I liked that he seemed to underestimate me, and overestimate himself. And after this latest blithe assumption of superiority, I couldn't help myself. I'd play along. But maybe – just maybe, I'd surprise him.

— Understand this though, I told him, thinking of those belligerent England fans in the pub – any trouble and I'm not covering your scrawny old arse. I will feed you straight – to the wolves.

He grinned, waving my stipulation away as if it was so much hot air. Certainly something was making his cheeks ruddy. From somewhere he'd found an old hairbrush of Karen's, and appeared to be cleaning it, drunkenly pulling long, fragile strands of hair from its bristles. I stood up and grabbed it away from him. It took a while, but finally I got him to the door. After we shook hands on our deal, he added:

— You understand you're paying for the petrol up there, yeah?

— Agreed. Up to a maximum of 50p?

He wasn't, I suppose, the only one who was a little merry.

That next morning, I should have had second thoughts; I saw the lower leaves of Karen's cheese plant had grown limp and yellow, as though having been dosed with something inimical to their health. Its pot sat right by the chair in which Harris had reclined the night before. The Vat 69, I'd thought when I first noticed: the old man had tipped his measure of paint stripper away.

It seemed an obvious explanation at the time. Back then I thought I knew enough about all sorts of things – houseplants, people, life.

4

Six a.m. the following Friday saw me out on the Chiswick borders. Harris was waiting outside the tube, as we'd agreed, in a beaten down LDV. Five minutes after that I was on the South Circular, gripping the huge, grimly functional steering wheel, my foot on a temperamental clutch the size of a pedal on a kiddie's trike. At first preoccupied with scratching at another disgusting-looking plaster around one of his fingers, Harris eventually found some relief, and set at a Day-Glo scotch egg the size of a softball – breakfast, apparently. He could barely speak through the cloying paste that squeezed between his teeth and gathered at the corners of his mouth, although that did nothing to stop him trying:

— I don' make this par-ticlar trip too offen; only when I'm certain... tha' there'll be enough goodies 'vailable.

By the time we reached the motorway, he was asleep. I forced the van doggedly up the middle lane of the M1, somehow managing to make Darlington by eleven. Our first few pick-ups were unremarkable – at each one we collected a small number of boxes from a rundown charity. All were small local affairs, nothing run at a national level, like Oxfam or British Heart Foundation places. At the fourth or fifth outlet – The Lambton and Skerne Defenders Trust, whatever that was – we loaded up more of the same. Only this time Harris was also handed an envelope from the till. I'd assumed that if money was going to change hands, it would be Harris paying for the stock, rather than the other way around.

It was difficult getting anything from Harris. Whatever subtle approach I made, he somehow twisted it about or gave outright bizarre replies. When I pushed at whether he expected to find much valuable or antiquarian stock during the trip, he pushed back, accusing me of being unable to handle such things. Of not having adequate storage conditions. Of being incapable of grading them correctly. Of not understanding the potential market. If I knew the first thing about the more valuable of the collectibles, he told me at one point, then I ought to know better than stacking them all up together on a bookshelf.

— They're like rats, he said. — If you leave them alone, they'll eat each other up.

— You mean fish, I said. — Tropical fish and the like.

He looked over at me, shaking his head.

— This is gold I'm giving you. Don't you want to write it down somewhere?

Only his tone was abject, banterless.

Eventually I just asked, flat out, about the envelope from the till. He shrugged.

— Man there owes me from before, Harris said.

We were back on the road by then, heading on to the next stop.

— What exactly does he owe you for?

I had tried to keep my tone light, casual and interested. But Harris only shrugged:

— That *your* business, is it?

The last consignment had appeared to be of rather inferior quality, piled up in old Seville and Granada orange boxes. Looking at the chestnut-brown speckles on their page edges as I loaded them up, I'd had to remind myself that Harris knew more than I did. But after seeing that he was being reimbursed for vanishing the stock, I began to think that there might be some other peculiar business afoot.

Somewhat irked by his answer, I slowed the van.

— Look. There's a bus stop up ahead. Shall I stop and fill up the back with the contents of the litter bin? Probably eBay that for more than the crap we just picked up.

I had expected him just to unleash one of his peculiar smiles and mutter something vaguely enigmatic: his default MO. But for some reason my comment riled him, and he snapped his answer:

— Oh, you needn't worry yourself about the junk; we'll be dumping most of it out in a couple stops... Sorry – *you'll* be dumping most of it out.

He looked tired, almost as though he hadn't slept the length of the M1. I, on the other hand, felt eagerly alive. The fact I'd needled him so cheaply felt like a victory. Even if I didn't get the whole picture of how he wangled his cheap job-lots, there would still be a chance to wind him up. And perhaps from that something interesting would slip.

But if that deal at the Trust was a puzzle, then our next stop, down towards Middlesbrough, was an outright mystery. We had arrived at the place, a detached, high-piled stack of Yorkshire sandstone halfway down a hilly residential street, and decamped immediately into a rather chilly, damp basement at the back of the building. I mentioned to Harris that it hardly seemed an ideal atmosphere for book storage, and in return he assigned me the task of carting a stack of foul-smelling canvas duffle bags from the van into the cellar.

— You planning on helping?

— I could, he said, but made no actual move to do so. That was about the level of his wit: a real funny fucker. I faked throwing one of the bags at him. He didn't flinch.

— What's in these, anyway?

Harris grasped exactly what I was angling at.

— It's either the finest Afghan black, or political dissidents smuggled in from Tibet. I'll check the paperwork and come back to you...

In truth I had already sneaked a look. Inside was nothing of any worth: old supermarket bags full of small pieces of junk paper – till receipts, old flyers, ticket stubs and the like. The contents were about as substantial as Harris's explanation.

There was that particular dank smell to the basement that some disused spaces have – a kind of mildewed scaliness. In a corner, just out of the tube lighting, I could make out the edges of a pair of flabby, pallid shapes – coverless bean bags, perhaps. What they looked like, crouched there in the shadows, were oversized mushrooms or giant, dirty meringues. Having seen them, I had immediately the forceful notion that they were responsible for the place's smell.

Yet they weren't all that was pale and silent. While investigating the duffles, I had been surprised by the young man overseeing the deal. He was the pathologically silent type, a watcher, his features hidden and eyes blown up cartoonishly by super-thick corrective lenses. Harris spoke dismissively to him on our arrival and following that lead, I pegged him as a nobody; possibly even a nobody *manqué*. The slump and bulge of his midriff was squeezed into a bottle-blue Lyle & Scott golf sweater, tight around his underdeveloped arms and short at the waist, revealing an unappetising swath of pallid, hair-flecked underbelly. There, at the top of the basement steps, against the backdrop of the flaking whitewash painted directly onto brick, he seemed so perfectly at home that I couldn't imagine him anywhere else.

Of course, he didn't say anything. Just watched with those unreal, magnified eyes of his. I stared back at him just long enough to let him know that I didn't care whether or not he'd seen me having a nose into the bags. But I wasn't the focus of his interest. His eyes were fixed on the scrap paper I had in my hand, looking at it with something like greed. And when I stuffed the paper back into the duffle, something about him deflated – as though he could have gotten any smaller. By the time I had climbed the steps, he was in the act of disappearing. Yet it was not the scuttling I had anticipated. It was more an evaporation – or dispersion, like a cloud of spore.

But when the odd little man – I had started to think of him as Lyle and Scott – and Harris reconvened, out by the van, I made sure I was right there next to them, to witness their reckoning up. I watched Harris fiddle with that dirty, sticky plaster of his, as he carried out his negotiations. There were a great many references made to someone called Aikman who, I inferred, was Lyle's boss. But that was as much as I could garner. When eventually he offered up a crumple of soiled tenners, Harris took and straightened them, then shook his head sadly.

— I'll have to take a couple back, then.

There was no question of the sad little man being able to haggle, and after a short burst of muted, almost wordless pleading, Harris ordered me to go and retrieve a pair of the duffle bags from the cellar.

— I'm not a cruel man, he added. — Grab the two smallest.

As though taking back only the most modest of the bags somehow counted as an act of magnanimity.

I told Harris to go himself.

— Now, that *is* cruelty, said Harris.

But when he wheezed off towards the basement, I pulled him back. That I'd be doing most of the physical work had been part of our understanding. After all, Harris wasn't a young man; now and then, he had a distant look in his eye, like he was busy with something else – something I thought might be the kissing of middle-age goodbye. Despite that, he could have shown a little more grace – or even gratitude – when it came to the hard work required.

— Come with me, I told Lyle, who was still pleading with – or rather, mewling at – Harris.

Down in the basement, I grabbed one of the duffles and yanked open its drawstring. I pulled out about a quarter of the contents – two or three big handfuls of scrap paper, and dumped it down on the big workbench with the other bags. I did the same with the other duffle.

I suppose I felt sorry for the man, although I couldn't look him in the eye. He was still there, snivelling in the dank gloom when I left. Although I had considered the possibility that the used receipts were part of some sophisticated fraud, large swathes of the paper seemed years old. And till ink – no doubt by design – fades quickly to illegibility. Thus, while I didn't have any idea what the used receipts and other crap were for, or why they might be worth anything to anybody, I was certain of something else: I didn't like being made complicit in Harris's bullying. Or perhaps it was simply that I wanted to undermine the old man: I was floundering, after all, in my efforts to puzzle out his money-making ruse. I had to remind myself that the actual aim was to scope out the exact provenance of the books – worthless or otherwise – that we were collecting. Everything else was just a distraction: perhaps even deliberate noise. I was beginning to understand that Harris was secretive, and certainly savvy – and perhaps just paranoid enough – to attempt a program of deliberate obfuscation.

Back out front I dumped the duffles at Harris's feet. He tried flinging them into the back of the van with what I assumed to be a flourish of venom. But the rancour reached no further than his face; his shoulders simply weren't up to the task: one of the bags rolled back out. I picked it up and tossed it in. It wasn't heavy – not all that much; this time it slammed against the far wall.

5

The next stop was a small commercial site, a collection of demi-warehouses and industrial units built out of new red brick, out in the hinterlands between Middlesbrough and Redcar. We pulled up outside Our Boro's Recycling, its wall sign cheap and nasty, better suited to a tattooist's, the usual triangle of green arrows twisted into a scaly tail-chasing dragon. Small-time writ large.

While we waited on the forecourt for his man to show, Harris started to go through the book-boxes, tossing a sizable proportion of the items into a rusty yellow skip. But even that seemed too much of an exertion for him. His pleated corduroys and heavy shirt were a lunatic choice on such a warm day, and he was soon sweating. When he began to cough, I suggested he take a break. The suggestion was ignored. Shortly after that, a man in a filthy boiler suit appeared. After greeting him, Harris turned to me, brandishing a folded twenty.

— See that Total garage we passed a wee skiff down the road?

I treated him to the flattest of all my facial expressions. His game was as plain as his sudden Scots was phony: getting rid of me while he discussed the terms of his arrangement or some other sensitive information, whatever that might have been. There was clearly some aspect of the deal that he didn't want to share. Or perhaps he was worried that his contact would clock me as a potential buyer – even offer me the chance to come and buy my own lot of stock.

I didn't intend to be put off so easily. So I complained a little at the inevitable request that I fill up the van's tank, before

39

adding, in a sullen voice, that I was going to grab a coffee while I was gone and wouldn't be hurrying back.

— Half an hour max, Harris warned me. — Then we *get*.

Slamming the van door was a nice touch – as was gunning the engine as I pulled away. But soon as I turned onto the access road, out of sight of the forecourt, I wheeled the old clunker about and parked up by the next unit along. My plan was to slip back and see what I could overhear, and then perhaps force an introduction. But Harris and the owner, or manager, or whoever he was, had already disappeared inside. The reception area wasn't especially receptive: the door didn't open and the huge roller shutter that allowed vehicular access into the building was padlocked. I punched the green metal roller; it rattled and then hissed. But as I rubbed my knuckles, I realised there was something else I could do.

This time as I drove up, I noticed the small tarnished plaque on the gatepost, crowded in by spears of privet: The Yokohama Centre for Creative and Art Therapies. The front door was unlocked, the interior cool and blue and silent. Summer holidays, I supposed. The loser in the blue Lyle & Scott looked genuinely surprised to see me. He jumped – or perhaps more accurately, twitched – as he poked out his head into the hallway. A notion, sharp and irresistible, arrived: I'd disturbed some shameful, solitary activity: a visit to some deviant internet quarter, most likely.

The smile and greeting that I thought might calm him – even charm him – only seemed to make those eyes of his grow even larger. Having reconciled myself to the possibility of having to pay him a small something to spill his guts, I felt pleasantly surprised, at least at first, when he threw them up – almost all over my feet. Out came a stream of nervous, chattering words. Clearly, public speech – or indeed any kind of speech – wasn't a primary talent. Did that explain why he was at the centre? If a therapy centre it was. There wasn't, as far as I could see, anyone else there. And although the interior had the feel of an institution – a certain sparseness, the neutral colours of the walls, the inoffensive artwork I could see hung along the hallway – there was no tell-tale signage, other than the half-hidden plaque on the gate, and no obvious reception or office. Yet then I looked at Lyle, stammering away, and I thought, surely: *surely.*

— He – he sent you back, didn't he? His hands wavered at chest level as if trying to push away rising water. But he couldn't stop his own flood:

— You can't have them. They're mine now. Go. Go away.

I held out the duffle I'd brought with me from the van.

— This is yours, I said. — Just tell me.

— Tell you what?

He had managed almost, that time, to sound half-cocky. It was to prove his high point.

I turned, making sure that the duffle swung close to him, and started away. It was almost too easy. He wouldn't want to lose out on so much precious scrap.

— Come back, he said, somewhat unnecessarily: I hadn't gone anywhere. Not yet.

— I just want you to explain, I said, looking back over my shoulder, — exactly why you're paying for this stuff.

But that demand left him tongue-tied. Some sort of internal struggle or qualm played out across his face before finally he nodded agreement. And once the duffle was in his hands, he led me down the wide hallway to the room he'd just quit.

Inside was a bureau, chairs and a long, lazy couch. It had the air of a consultation room. He shook out the contents of

the bag onto the desktop and grabbed up a couple of the papers – tickets or dockets, I didn't really see. I didn't *see* because
immediately he stuffed them into his mouth and began chewing.

His lips moved quickly; every now and then there was a
soft plash. All the while he kept raised to mine those huge,
magnified eyes, which were both weak and somehow defiant
at the same time. A dribble of cloudy saliva escaped the corner
of his mouth. He closed his mouth, swallowed, and then out
into his hand spat a clump of sodden paper. It was whitish,
with seams of dirty ink here and there: impacted, incoherent
type. He held it out for my inspection, his eyes still unmoving.

Not until he had moved beyond the bureau did I realise
that there was something else in the room with us as well. Back
there, in the space behind the desk's swivel chair, was a pallid
shape. For a horrid moment, I thought it a large, white dog.
But I remembered then the bloaty white masses in the basement; they hadn't been mushrooms at all. What I had seen, I
now guessed, was the backs of sculptures – figures like this one
– down on all fours. This one was clumsily formed, with somewhat elephantine limbs, but recognisable – just – as a human
figure. Or so the shape and mass of the head and neck suggested.

Lyle bent over. He pressed his lump of paper against the
sculpture's hidden underside. On the carpet beneath was a
sheet of plastic, from which he picked up a spattered palette
knife, using the flat of the blade to smooth off the mashed
paper. His lack of talent for life was mirrored in his ability to
produce art – if that was what such a thing could be termed.
This, I guessed, was some form of therapy, but why the use of
Harris's waste paper should be important, I didn't know. The
little man was absorbed in forming a pair of what had to be

rather pendulous breasts, positioned far too close to the figure's waist. Thus engrossed in his pushing and shaping, he appeared to have altogether forgotten my presence.

There was other hopelessly inept detailing: an attempt at wormy strands of hair, worked around the crown and chin, and the same again between the legs – features that reinforced my impression that the piece was sexualized, if rather bizarrely so. I had the creeping sensation that my initial flip judgment – that I had interrupted Lyle's browsing of pornography – hadn't in some sense been far from the truth. But whatever – I had seen enough – enough to realise that the little man was, in some profound way, deeply unwell. So before he could catch me up again in that glassy, cradling gaze of his, or offer me anything else, I turned and slipped out the door.

As I went, I heard spit and splatter – the coughing up of another piece of the papier-mâché out and onto the figure. But the further away I got, the more what I had heard began to form words in my brain. It was, I thought, what Lyle had been trying to tell me all along, a stony little nub of defiance that he kept brilliantly hidden away:

— I'm happy. I'm happy *now*.

Could anyone really believe that?

6

Back at the recycling centre, Harris had negotiated the collection of a huge cling-wrapped pallet of books. Unfortunately, we had to strip it down a foot or so and then rewrap before we could see it fit, fork-lifted up, into the rear of the LDV. The stress of negotiations – what else could it have been? – was still all about Harris's face: cheeks reddened by exertion, eyes glassy. And, even as I was glad he hadn't noticed – or at least hadn't commented on – my tardiness in returning, I felt irked as well. As much as anything else, I realised, I had wanted to rile him. Instead I had just wasted my time on the little side jaunt; I had learned nothing of any importance. I had only gone so as to feel I was doing something of my own accord, as opposed to being shunted hither and thither at Harris's whim.

We visited another ten or twelve rundown charities, making our way down the coast to Whitby. Our collections were made from well-weathered faces, ageing women with a certain brightness that held together the disparate elements of their appearance: the uncut hair, perhaps silver or white, perhaps dyed; the tombstone teeth, perhaps lightly nicotined; the neat grey austerity of trim cardigans, possibly skimmed – at a fair price, of course – from their donations; the stertorous breath and the bright, tidy necklaces: the clean, shimmering crucifixes, small and expensive, more handsome than any other facet of their bearers' appearance. But for all that, there was almost always concern and kindness in both their eyes and manner. Unnecessarily so: could they really think that I would damage myself lifting their little boxes of books?

I quickly learned to anticipate our hosts' likely concerns: pigeons out the back, rodents in the storeroom, shoplifters in the front, the theft of donations left outside when the shops were closed, Eastern European and African faux-charities competing for stock.

I asked directly how Harris made his contacts. The question, met with a frigid silence, felt about as welcome as sand in a prophylactic. Even so, I persisted:

— That last place, say? How did you meet the manager – Martha, wasn't it?

— How did I meet her? His face was stony. — By walking in the fucking door.

I'd started to glimpse in Harris what I thought of as a second, shadow personality. The dominant side of him enjoyed banter and refused to give anything away other than wind-ups. That Harris liked – *loved* – lording it over me. Yet there was another one as well, this one cooler – no, *colder*. This one practised no sort of friendliness, superficial or otherwise. To be totally honest, he scared me a little. But he did give direct answers. Responses so straight-up, so literal, that they seemed almost autistic in character. At first I thought it was just another wind-up strategy, but the flashes of that shadow self were so rare and unpredictable, I began to wonder... I realised that I'd need to watch him all the more carefully.

There seemed to be no consistent logic to the nature of his arrangements – at some shops he filled out forms, at others he just thrust a handful of notes at the women, yet others seemed to be trades. Mostly, the books seemed to be given away to us freely. And some of our stops entailed, after a quick chat, no business at all. Occasionally, Harris collected money – sometimes for drop-offs, sometimes for collections.

Only at our last stop of the day – a cat rescue outfit in

Whitby – did anything different happen. The shop was crammed into a long thin room, with only the tiniest of display windows built into the twee, pale stone frontage. It was crushed in between a Greggs and a building society. They had only a single shelf of books available for sale; the rest had been set aside in a tiny upstairs stock room crammed with clothes rails and pallid mannequin spares.

— The tacky crap is what sells, the manager told me. I assumed she meant bric-a-brac, of which there was plenty out on display.

We were upstairs by then, Harris – surprise, surprise – nowhere to be seen. It had been a crush making it up the narrow staircase. Anna – she had introduced herself with a clear, bell-like voice – was nearly as tall as me, and considerably wider. But in contrast to the frail, unworldly dears that had been clucking over me all afternoon, she was something of a relief: shrewd and confident. It was a relief, in all honesty, talking to someone normal.

— Take 'em and good rid, she told me as I lifted the first box.

There were about twenty boxes in all, and by the time I'd shifted all but two of them out to the van, I'd lost a little skin from my knuckles. The unclad stone of the narrow stairwell was not kind.

I was upstairs having a little curse to myself when Anna stepped out from behind a rail of unsorted clothing, and stood looking at me, her arms crossed. And although she was younger than me – in her twenties, I thought – I felt quite sure that I was being appraised.

— Not seen you before, she said.

— Just doing my bit for *Help the Aged*, I said, gesturing vaguely with my thumb in the direction we had last seen

Harris.

— Right.

She smiled then, as though I was something of an idiot. But perhaps she reconsidered:

— Well, Mr Assist-a-Pensioner, there's something here I'd like you to look at.

Twenty seconds later, I had a rather attractive copy of Mallory's *Le Morte D'Arthur* in my hands. It was a sixty-year old reprinting of an earlier edition. The illustrations were by Aubrey Beardsley, and the book itself was well preserved. I cooed my appreciation.

— Worth a little something, isn't it? asked Anna.

I thought that it would probably go for around a hundred pounds – and said as much.

— Well, us won't get that in here, will we?

I told her that she could take it to a reputable book-dealer. An honest one might consider selling it on commission – given that it was for a charity.

Anna just laughed and shook her head.

— You needn't make pretend with me, she said. — Take it – it's for the *children*.

For a moment, I didn't know what she meant. And then suddenly, a horrible possibility came to me: Harris was collecting the books under false pretences.

Stalling for time to think, I riffled the pages. It was then I noticed that the front endpapers were filled with handwriting in a faded, watery brown ink. Notes, perhaps even scholarly ones. My assumption was that they would make the book greatly less saleable – unless some sap might believe that Tolkien or Lewis or some lesser Inkling had made the annotations. I winced as the thought occurred. Harris was getting to me. I was already starting to think as he did. Or rather, as I *imagined* that he did.

Anna had seen me looking at the scribbles. Oddly, she seemed to think that they added value to the book: from the way she spoke, it almost seemed that it was the annotations themselves that I would be interested in.

— Look, she said. — I can see you're a right good fellow and all... If it makes it easier for you, just buy the book from us. That way, we'll get something as well.

Her voice had grown small and demure and pleading. Everything she hadn't, up until that point, been. I fell for it. From my pocket I fumbled a twenty, the first note I could find.

— God bless you, she said, taking it smoothly away from me.

Except that I wasn't quite sure it was God she had asked for the blessing. It had sounded another word altogether. But that had to have been the work of her accent, and the clumsiness of my ears.

— You should probably finish up, she reminded me gently, her eyes switching over to the remaining few boxes.

That was a good suggestion; a very short while later, Harris reappeared. I popped the Mallory inside the box I was carrying; Anna, I noted, made no mention of it to Harris. Out in the van, I slipped it into my bag. After all, it wasn't part of the general stock now; I was the one who had paid for it. I suppose if the whole little deal hadn't flustered me so, I might have thought to wonder why Anna hadn't offered the book directly to Harris, or just let it go along with all the other stock.

As we left the shop, Harris ahead of me and impatient to leave, I spoke quietly to Anna.

— Look, I said, — If it turns out to be worth something, I'll split whatever I get for it with you. I've got the address here

– I'll send on a cheque.

She waved the offer away, the look on her face almost pitying. She didn't believe for a moment that I would. Before I could turn away though, something peculiar happened.

I thought, even at the time, that I imagined it.

Anna's tongue, all coated with an odd sickly verdigris, flickered out over her lips. Something obscene and suggestive coiled eel-like in the wet of her eye.

And then she was saying ta-ra, calling me pet, all hint of impropriety gone, the only inflection in her voice that buoyant, municipal friendliness.

7

The bleak, heavy sun and the work I'd put in meant that by
the time we reached Scarborough, I was beyond ready for the
cold beer that Harris had been promising all the long drive
through the moors. We dumped the van outside our lodgings.
Harris knew the owner well, he said, but she wouldn't yet be
home from work: we had to collect the key from the local
newsagents.

Although it was unmarked as such, there could be no
doubting that the big old house was a bed-and-breakfast. The
interior smelled like it had been deep-fried; the carpeting was
equally delicious – a patterning of shit-brown moths crushed
onto khaki ground by asymmetric, crisscrossing grids. While
I scoped the leatherette lounge suite and the narrow patio
windows with their flaking paint, Harris scrawled a note. We
stood in the kitchen, listening through the double glazing left
locked on its trickle vent to the dying sounds of the summer
afternoon – insects and the song of the martins, children's faint
laughter foaming somewhere in the distance. Beyond that, and
softest of all, was sea-sound, a distant, flailing tambourine.

I told Harris he needed to do the decent thing, and get me
to the pub.

§

Our first pair of pints disappeared quickly.

— Get what you wanted today? Harris asked. He directed
his question into the air above the bar, where he stood, a
folded ten erect between index and middle.

— All I want, I lied, — is the books we agreed on.

I didn't like that Harris had decided to ambush me with this, but I wasn't going to lose my nerve. He couldn't see through me, I *knew* he couldn't. Fishing, that was all.

— Not ambitious, then?

I looked at him. Straight bat, I thought. We *were* in Yorkshire, after all.

— Just a way to make a little bit of easy money, I told him.

— If you want *easy*, I could push some errands your way. Now and again. Nothing strenuous.

I chuckled. Harris'd had his go. Now I pushed back:

— A job? Working for you? What would be the weekly rate of compensation: a whole pallet of worthless pulp-ready crap?

— Crap? Harris was grinning.

I nodded. — Collected a lot of it today.

— Aye, he said, his diction doing one of those odd ground-shifts. — Wait 'til tomorrow. There'll be sparkles a-plenty.

I needled a bit more, about the duffle bags full of scrap paper that he'd sold to Lyle, perhaps a couple of other obscurities. This time, I had the result I wanted.

— Exactly what is it you think you want to know? His voice was far too loud, as if he had been facedown at the sup for hours. I moved slightly away from him.

— I'll know when I hear it.

I next asked if we'd be turning in from the coast the following day. Surely we'd surely be taking in York?

That assumption seemed to amuse Harris.

— York? The fuckers there are so tight-arsed, their strategy is to sit on their books til they transfigure into diamonds.

An unlikely way to run a business, I told him.

— They just cut up tourists, he said, his voice a hoarse

pseudo-whisper.

— Scuttle scat on the gullible. Muuuurcans or Konnichi-wa. Probably looking right now to expand into duping – sorry, I mean trading *with* – Shenzhen, or Guangdong, or wherever *their* nouveau-riche congregate.

I nodded as if I knew all about it, glancing over at him.

Harris was still in the clothes he'd had on all day – the off-white shirt and dark pleats that at a distance looked plain. Only close-up did you catch the luxury of the weave, the subtly needled embroidery, the ivory buttons. I remember thinking that that those clothes meant money.

We took another beer apiece, standing at the bar, working one another over. Finally I felt ready to ask:

— Who are these children I've been hearing about?

That must have been the only time I ever saw uncertainty, or anything like it, pay a visit to his face. It didn't stay long.

— Que? he said. As though that had ever been witty.

The obfuscation was too late; I'd already seen him.

— The ones we're collecting for.

He muttered something under his breath. It sounded like *silly bitch*.

— You've misunderstood, he said then. — Look. People work in these places – in these shops – for a reason. You know all about the old ones – the ones who just do it to get outside somewhere. Others just can't get on anywhere else – they're too slow, too unreliable, too whatever. Charities aren't necessarily just about the cause up there on the shopfront. There are some people who work in the sector because, without putting too fine a point on it – they're *fucking* crazy.

We both knew whom he was talking about, although neither of us had mentioned Anna by name.

— And you? Are you crazy? I asked, mostly just to keep

him talking.

— No. Are you simple?

— Give me one good reason I shouldn't just go out to that van right now and drive myself back to London.

The very idea amused him.

— You're already drunk, he said. — And it's *my* van. And technically, legally – whatever – the stuff inside belongs to me. And really, what would be the point? You've already done most of the hard work. It gets easy from hereon in...

As the sentence dangled, I showed him that he wasn't the only one who could conjure a smile that spelt c-u-n-t:

— And yet... I'm the one holding the keys. It's still early: still time to spruce myself up. *I* could be home tonight...

We looked at each other then. I remember thinking that Harris looked almost happy. His mouth was flat, but all the same: he was enjoying himself. So was I.

— Who *are* the children?

— There aren't, he said, — any kiddies.

— I know that. The question is: does everyone we've collected books from know it?

— Shit, said Harris, his face breaking at last into a grin. — Half.

— Half of them know?

— No. An even split: half of the books. For you. That's what this is about, isn't it?

— So that's an admission?

— Done just to shut you up, you nagging old hen. No one thinks we're collecting for charity. You might be the only one... You should have, he said, jabbing his finger at me — asked for half from the off. There's little enough money in your game as it is.

— So why are you in it, old cock?

53

— That's something else you should have asked before now. The books? He paused, did something funny with his face, as though trying to suck a sliver of meat from between his teeth. — A side line: it defrays costs.

— What's the fucking main line then?

The matter of Lyle came to mind – but I didn't see how the wretched clutch of notes he'd handed to Harris could ever add up to any kind of serious money. I hadn't, at that point, understood that I was asking altogether the wrong questions. I even thought, with my pressing about the children, that I'd actually forced something from him – some small tab of respect.

— Keep setting them up, Harris said, gesturing at the beer taps. — If I knock enough down I suppose I might mistakenly enlighten you further...

And after a moment, he added:

— There's really something else you should be more concerned about...

I waited for the punchline. When it arrived, it was suitably disappointing:

— You should be asking how you might convince me to go easy on you.

Clearly, he fancied himself as a something of a drinker. I tried not to mock as I asked:

— Now, why would you want to go hard...?

The odd thing about the timing of the ghost voicemail was that Harris was just then trying to nudge our conversation towards Karen; he'd been trying on and off all day. I hadn't finished reading *Under the Volcano*, and remembering the old man's interest, I'd brought my copy along on the trip – a little something with which to bait him.

Earlier on in the day, just after lunch, I'd had a few minutes to myself while the old man sloped off, likely for his postprandial extrusion. Sat behind the wheel, I opened the book. The heat of the afternoon and the stuffiness of the cab saw me napping before I'd even read a single page. I awakened to find Harris back in his seat, examining the strip of photographs serving as my bookmark with an odd, slightly lecherous interest.

— Your children would be beautiful.

Teeth showed through beard. It was difficult to say which were greyer. I snatched the photos from his hand.

Since then he had made a number of allusions to Karen; I had at some point made the mistake of telling him her name, and he'd pounced on it, toying with its pronunciation like a half-interested tom batting at a giddy, stunned mouse.

It started up once again in the pub that evening, not long after Harris had agreed to increase my share of the books. He'd had enough by then, to risk familiarity:

— She's going to leave you, he said. — You do know that, don't you? They all do it, sooner or later...

Sensing the possibility that he might be gearing up to make some awful, beer-sodden outpouring of personal woe, I looked away, catching our reflection in the mirror behind the bar. The gleam of the lingering summer day silhouetted us, and I was surprised to see how tall Harris appeared next to me. I stood up straight and took a swallow from my glass.

— She's already gone, I told him. — Married to her job.

I'd be damned before he had a thing to hold over me, so I served him up the worst – the most definitely untrue – interpretation.

— Alterations, he countered, as if talking about a suit. — A snip or tuck. Trim out what you don't like. What you don't need. Rewrite the whole sad story.

But before I could tell him exactly *how* he needed to fuck off (my requirements were that it should be immediate, painful, and preferably entail a later, awkward visit to a medical professional), my phone started to shake and sting: the staccato, vamped intro to *Strange Brew*, my voicemail alert.

It was too good an opportunity to squander. Without letting Harris see what I was doing (even if he was almost certainly ignorant of the workings of any phone produced since the millennium had turned), I connected to the messaging service, and took a step away from the bar.

— Sorry, I told him, as though it were an actual call. — I need to take this one.

My plan was to take as long as I could. I wanted Harris to stew over what I'd laid on him re Anna and the children. Plus, I just wanted a break. There was something very wearing about his company.

But by the time I'd managed to find a quiet spot at the bottom of the beer garden, I was confused.

The message that my voicemail had described as new, was anything but. It was an old message from Karen. And not one of which I wanted particularly to be reminded. I wasn't even sure that I'd saved it. At least not purposefully: the message had been left in the heat of a long-distance argument. I remembered quite clearly listening to it the first time round – there had been a peculiar distortion on the line, a hum, or buzzing. Karen's voice had been – and *was* again – tiny, but not any the less sharp for that. After I heard it through, I spent a little time going through the options, checking the other saved messages, just to make sure I hadn't somehow missed the phantom *new* message that I'd expected.

But there was nothing.

And finally, I killed the connection, only to find that Harris had shadowed me outside, and was standing waiting at a nearby table. He'd brought my pint with him, which I promptly jammed down before demanding we move on. The pub garden was full of birdsong and idiocy, the chirruping of voices too much like the one I'd just canned.

8

Our next stop was called The Anchor, the sort of dour drinker being crushed slowly out of London. In the time it took me to buy drinks, Harris managed to upset the four young men at the pool table with some stray comment about their undercooked facial hair. Somehow though, after a conversation which had seemed to me charged with the menace of physical violence, one of the group (polo-shirted, perhaps not the most vocal, but certainly a, if not *the*, string-puller) had fetched Harris a pint of lager from the bar. It felt too close of a squeeze and so, mindful that he had form in magicking up confrontation, I dragged him off to one of the hidey-holes in the snug.

We'd not been seated five minutes before Harris started to scratch about on the dusty moss velour of our bench's cushion. He lifted his discovery up to the light: a long flaccid hair, silver-gold in the lamplight, mousy-brass out of it.

— You don't want to think again?

— About?

— My offer. Come and do a bit for me...

He was still dangling the hair, watching it intently. Not once since finding it had he even glanced at me.

— I don't need a job.

— No, replied Harris, as though he was in fact agreeing with me. — What you need is a *place*. Somewhere you fit in.

I rolled my eyes, but Harris wasn't giving up:

— I could use a – librarian? An archivist?

I threw back the rest of my beer and slammed the pint glass down on the table.

— On to the next one.

Harris still had most of the extra pint – Stella, according to the glass's decal – that young Fred Perry had brought to him. His beard, rather than his mouth, seemed to be doing the drinking when he supped at the glass.

— Aye, he said. — I know just the ticket. Somewhere a touch less crabby, I think. Somewhere we needn't worry about the bell at the bar...

Our move was indeed a swerve in a more gentrified direction although, perhaps unsurprisingly, the place proved far from flush with welcome. The little hotel looked as though it had been recently emboutiqued and once inside, Harris blinked tearfully at the shabby-chic reception area. He'd promised me that he knew both place and proprietor well. Clearly, to him at least, the new 'old' look represented a betrayal.

We waited a long time for anyone to show; the girl who eventually attended us said that she was sorry that we'd not only had to wait but that she didn't have any rooms, either. It was the sort of sorryness entailing no hint of apology.

— Where's Queenie? Harris asked.

A creaking came from the armpits of his leather jacket as he stood swaying slightly. The day's warmth hadn't much receded and even with the arrival of evening, he was still overdressed. A film of greasy-looking sweat covered his forehead, and a thick blue worm of a vein distended one temple. I felt then – and certainly not for the first time that day – embarrassed by his company.

— Queenie? he repeated.

The woman looked at him as though he'd asked if he could take her then and there over the tiny escritoire that served, rather ridiculously, as a reception desk. She shook her head:

— Sorry. I thought you said...

Harris raised an eyebrow. There could be no doubt of it: he wasn't smiling. His eyes were bloodshot and he looked pained.

— Queenie? Harris said again. — *Kwee*-knee.

— I don't know what that is, said the girl, her voice starting to betray irritation.

Harris reached over the desk and plucked a piece of branded memo paper from a block sitting in an expensive-looking brass holder. From somewhere he'd found a fountain pen, which he used to stroke rapidly across the paper.

His fingers moving rapidly, he folded the memo into a shape resembling a tri-point crown, and without pausing, pressed it onto the girl; she didn't want to take it, yet Harris knew exactly how to offer it to ensure that it ended up in her hands. Precisely how he did it, I don't know. It seemed as though I was continuously looking at the wrong thing, and missing something that was happening somewhere else. It was Harris's face, for example, that caught my eye just then. I couldn't decide whether the expression on his face was a sneer or a leer.

Either way, I sensed we were about to be asked to leave.

I was wrong.

— When was the last time you were – here? she asked, smiling for the first time.

— Your bar, said Harris. — Is it open?

She shook her head, her nose wrinkling as though trying to suppress the smile below.

— Can it be? asked Harris.

— Guests only, the girl said, touching the folded crown to the corner of her mouth. She couldn't be flirting with him, could she? That seemed all too obscene; too implausible.

Her words were in fact the precursor to our admission:

two minutes later, we were tucked into a low-lit booth, with a view out onto the distant, darkening sea. In the slow summer dusk, the horizon line was still visible – just. Harris paid it no attention. He was too busy muttering to himself: he wanted, apparently, to make someone pay.

— Not me, I hope.

— Not you, he confirmed, apparently disgusted at the thought.

And then he began to retch. A glob of what looked like chowder, leavened with amber beer, shot out from between his fingers. He made a short series of liquidy barks then a sound as though sanding his throat with wet glasspaper. Finally, with an unhurried calm, he wiped his hands on the fronds of a nearby pot plant.

I smiled to myself. I thought that there might be plenty he could be persuaded to explain. And after that, Harris began to talk more freely. He held his liquor well, at least in one sense: there was no slurring of speech or much in the way of other physical indicators – other than his actual vomiting – but his conversation lurched from topic to occult topic.

At some point he led me out to the fringes of astrophysical speculation, specifically the rather outré notion that black holes were nothing other than the sites of the parallel universes suggested by a particular interpretation of quantum physics.

— Of course, Harris said then, with an oh-so-clever smile, — that notion itself is little more than a retread of a Gnostic idea.

He waited for me to ask more. For some unknowable reason, I was slow to respond.

— Certain sects prohibited representational art, deeming it a kind of blasphemy – a hubristic attempt to create other orderly worlds. The point being the physical location…

I'd stopped paying attention. Suddenly Harris lurched forward across the black marble table top, holding his hand out as if a pontiff offering his ring. It took a moment for me to make out, under the recessed ceiling spotlight, and its small bright reflection on the shiny black surface, exactly what I was supposed to be looking at. He'd torn away the plaster, revealing the cut I'd half-glimpsed during our meeting in the charity shop. It went all the way around his finger, a band of red-brown-pinky pain, with flushed edges, the skin shiny where it had begun to heal, dirty with scabbing in other places.

— What you need is a strip of skin, he was saying, — a strip that forms a – a – a continuous… ring. There are only so many places you can take it from.

He was grinning now.

— It mustn't be too large; or too small. It needs to be just – right. Finger or thumb…

And then we were interrupted by the bartender, telling us that they were about to close up the main doors; we were welcome to stay on but once we went out again – for a cigarette, or whatever – that would be it. Harris pulled his hand back slightly from underneath the spotlight whilst moving his other finger to point at his mouth as though pondering what to do; his movement so practised it seemed natural. It was only because I was slightly tipsy myself, paying only partial attention, that I noticed. That was how stage magicians were caught out, I remembered reading somewhere: they relied on having your full attention to practise the art of misdirection, and the bored, the drunk, the inattentive were the stuff of a nightmare audience.

Harris's mouth was moving. I caught a glimpse of it and again it seemed like something I shouldn't have seen. His lips that had seemed so perfectly drawn, now in their uneasy motion looked out of place, like slugs easing their way across a pristine dinner service.

— Scotch, said Harris's voice, casually indifferent to the movement his mouth was making. — What malts do you carry?

The barman coughed up the names: his struggle with pronunciation seeming to echo Harris's earlier retching fit. Harris, for his part, looked bored. As though he'd heard it all before.

— Bring us the one you think best, he said. — Bring the whole fucking bottle.

The man suggested that Harris give him a card to leave behind the bar.

— I'd be delighted, dear boy; but please, if anyone asks for me, you needn't let on that I'm in...

Harris was proffering a business card between two fingers: signally not the type of card to which the bartender had been referring. I was certain that our server would find some way – with the immaculate delicacy of manners he'd brought to bear so far – of conveying the more likely meaning of his reference. Instead he simply took the little cardboard oblong, disappearing it away into his apron, before ambling off in pursuit of our bottle.

While we waited for the man's return, Harris took it upon himself to show me what a Möbius band was and how to make one – he'd retrieved a newspaper from somewhere and, with a swift and rather unnerving accuracy, tore a sheet of it into a series of amazingly regular strips. And once the scotch had arrived, Harris was quickly to work: he was a devil for pouring the stuff. His actually drinking it isn't at all clear in my recollection, but he seemed constantly to be coaxing out the very leanest of measures, turning the glass into which he poured exactly as he twisted away the bottle, never wasting a drop.

After the first couple drams, I knew that the time had come: I asked him exactly what his main line of business was. For some reason I couldn't stop my cheeks bunching, threatening to push my lip out like a tearful schoolboy.

Harris didn't answer straight away. He picked up the bottle of whisky. Its label bore curlicued, uninterpretable Gaelic, reminding me of the original paperback cover for *Riddley Walker*, styled like a medieval illuminated manuscript. A minute splash of scotch plipped babyishly as it landed in my glass. And after a moment Harris raised his finger as though preparing to make a point, or as if to complain about my impertinence. But he caught himself. And answered my question:

— Favours, he said. — Favours.

He paused before adding:

— And the things I can get *from* books.

— Knowledge? I asked.

It sounded stupid. But the question for some reason annoyed Harris, perhaps even disturbed him, for his face suddenly tightened.

— You wanted to know about the children, he said. And now he did sound drunk. — Watch…

He poured a dribble of whiskey onto the surface of the newspaper Möbius strip he'd made earlier. His right ring finger traced its way clumsily along the band.

— It's a continuous surface, he said.

— And?

— And? Once you start down that road, there's no getting off…

But that was too opaque; and I told him as much. He looked back at me as though trying to decide whether I was

64

an incompetent. Eventually he decided that rather than explanation, what I needed was further detail:

— Of course, you wouldn't use scotch. Your surface less
absorbent. The serum more viscous…

He stared at me, daring that I ask more. But I didn't. And
when he continued, it occurred to me that I'd at last got the
better of him; he had to be more inebriated than I, and impatient enough that he couldn't outwait me. Even that small
victory made me glad; it held out the promise that I might yet
salvage some benefit from our little expedition.

— One part of the solvent should be blood.

His voice tapered to a whisper:

— You'll have some on hand if you've been careful, from
the cut made to remove the skin. But that's not all. You'll need
an equal part of sea –

The bartender reappeared at that moment, picked up the
bottle and poured another slug of whisky into each of our
glasses. Perhaps we weren't drinking up quickly enough for
him.

But the interruption soured Harris's mood. He scowled at
the man's retreating back, and wouldn't be drawn any further
on his little occult demonstration; I had been expecting some
final punchline or outcome, the natural finale to what I had
assumed to be little more than an arcane pub trick, Harris's
equivalent of striking a match one-handed or knocking a coin
through a table. As it was I hadn't the first idea of what he had
intended. When I asked directly, he replied,

— Why don't you fucking Google it?

I had baited him earlier about using a phone to check the
going price of books on Amazon or eBay. Clearly he hadn't
forgotten:

— You should be careful though…

Harris appeared now to be fully and manifestly drunk:

— Said you should *be careful* though.

— Why's that?

— Because... asking questions about this sort of thing...

— Yes?

— There are a lot of bad sorts here and about. Should be careful you don't pick up something nasty...

— You mean like a computer virus.

— *Worse* than a – virus. He smiled and reached up a hand to tap my temple. — Something that – installs itself – up here – on this hard drive...

— Okay...

— Or worse yet, on this one...

He spread his hand, indicating, I guessed, the world at large.

But even as I shook my head, laughing at the claim, I realised that the joke was on me: he'd taken a strip of newspaper and fastened it around my neck without my having noticed.

Harris winked and with a voice noticeably less slurred, said:

— Bee tee double-ewe, that's what they call close-up conjuring, net-boy.

But despite his little victory, I didn't think he was really fully in control; there was still a glassiness to his gaze.

— Remember. There are two kinds of props, he was telling me with a kind of hectoring seriousness. — Are you paying attention? I'm telling you something here. *Two kinds*. One – one kind of prop *is* the trick. The other kind – the *other* kind – conceals the workings of your trick. Drags the attention away. Do you see? I want you to understand.

He tried smiling at me; it was a hideous sight. Any sincerity he intended contributed only to the red, sweaty grin of a man who had drunk too much to pay proper regard to social niceties. I had much preferred his taking the piss.

Anyway, the outline of the evening from then on – already foggy – becomes mostly obscure, with little sharp peaks of memory showing through here and there. I wasn't the only one adrift, however. I remember returning to our lodgings where Harris, evidently stupefied, paused at the top of the first set of stairs, trying to unlock a lockless bedroom with keys supposed to open only the front door. Unsurprisingly that took forever, and annoyed, I pointed out the inanity of his action – no doubt too loud. For in short order the door shot open, revealing our landlady who clearly had retired some while before. Her greeting wasn't unfriendly; she simply directed us to our beds.

— Don't worry, Harris told her. — You're missing out on nothing; we're away the now. To nod. Off to nod. Tired like the dogs we are.

His voice boomed horribly in the little landing, the wood and plaster and wallpaper quite unable to constrain its distorted volume. And I remember quite distinctly the house appearing exceptionally small, a three-quarter-size mock up. But then, perhaps my senses weren't to be fully trusted, for everything at that point seemed to be floating, somehow un-anchored.

No, that was it. I was drunk.

My ears were buzzing: away to nod it was.

Morning hit hard, too early and too bright, a white sheet of light laced all around with Harris's snoring. I hadn't realised we were to share the attic room until I was too drunk to care. It was, no doubt, in order to save money. But then how much had we pissed away the night before? I had an uncertain recollection of Harris settling with the bartender at the hotel. Perhaps he had cashed a cheque, or got money back on his card, because I saw quite clearly the man open the register and count out a series of notes – orange-brown tens – which he fanned theatrically before squaring on the bar and passing to Harris.

The thought of that place, with its oak-and-leather smell aroma, conjured only nausea, and I pressed my eyes shut – to little result. The two windows in the little room, although rather mean in dimension, let in through their flimsy curtains a disproportionate amount of light. They had to be east-facing. I could hear the distant squawk and squabble of gulls. The sloping eaves felt as though they were pressing down on me. It was only after I'd found the bathroom and gulped down several mouthfuls of suspiciously chemically-tasting water straight from the tap that I was able to fall back, my head hidden beneath the sweaty polyester coverlet, into something that approximated sleep.

When I came up again, Harris was gone. It was close on eleven and the sun had powered into the sky, making what had previously been an atmosphere of slight discomfort into a broiling hell. It was only then that I thought to wonder, with impeccable hungover mislogic, if he wasn't also pocketing a kickback for us staying there, up in the loft of

Terylene Towers.

The downstairs was empty but just as I was considering getting out and finding a café for the cooked breakfast my body demanded, I heard someone on the stairs. The tall woman with hennaed hair coming down didn't fit well with my recollection of the doughy face that Harris had greeted at the top of the stairs the night before. But apparently it was she, transformed by daylight and makeup. We reintroduced ourselves; her name was Angie – or Ange – and she had me sit down in the kitchen.

— If you can hold fire for five, I'll have your breakfast on the go.

Harris, apparently, had gone out to meet someone about stock; he'd be back soon enough, she said. I supposed that was right: he'd turn up for me when some actual work needed doing.

Without asking, Angie banged a cup of tea down in front of me, preloaded with sugar. I sucked gratefully at it, and watched as she cooked. She was in her forties at least, I thought, the best part of her hidden away beneath a bandaging of dark rayon and the glam end of knitwear, traces of sparkling thread through black polycotton; she put me in mind of an archetypal biker's 'old lady' from those trashy late sixties Corman flicks, the mothering kind, only with extra kohl. But even the greasepaint couldn't quite hold her features together, wide eyes shooting off at slightly out-of-kilter angles, and a mouth that looked as though it had been hooked at either corner. She gave me a smile though – as she placed the plate on the table in front of me – that pulled all the pieces together: and suddenly, I felt right. Or at least at ease.

I didn't even mind when she sat down opposite me and unloaded her Superkings and Bic. So busy was I with the fried breakfast that even the plumes of her smoke couldn't quash my appetite. No doubt I didn't smell so great myself; I hadn't showered. Was that why she had lit up so nonchalantly? It only occurred to me then that the place was in fact her home. She'd just fed me, and could do whatever she pleased. I personally hadn't paid her a penny, whatever her arrangement with Harris.

Once finished, I took my plate over to the sink and slipped it into the washing-up water. Outside a pair of wasps circled, throwing themselves determinedly at the pane; despite their anger, there was something lulling and hypnotic in their buzzing, the distant side of the glass. Yet another joined them. Perhaps there was a nest nearby. Beyond them, towards the end of the long garden, the plain, flat lawn gave way to more unruly grass, grown dense and unctuous in the tall shade of a neighbour's leylandii. A number of pallid, rounded shapes loomed up out of the blue shadows. The things formed, I thought, some sort of a playset – a climbing frame and hut, swings and slide? It wasn't easy to see exactly, but they seemed to take the form of friendly woodland characters – cartoonish trees, squirrels, or rabbits – their colours bleached out by long exposure to the elements.

— You've got kids? I asked, nodding towards the playset at the end of the garden.

— Children? Ange asked, sucking in smoke. — Jesus. She coughed. — Children, parents. Didn't tell you a thing, did he?

Something hid behind her mordancy – an eagerness to talk, I felt. But how to nudge her?

I think I remembered to smile before asking:

— Is he getting something for us staying here?

I had no real grasp of how such an arrangement might work. But that didn't matter. Ange ignored my query, coming over to the sink, almost barging me out of the way.

After a moment she clarified – but another thing altogether, as it happened:

— There aren't any children here. Go sit down and I'll bring you another cup of tea.

Whatever had annoyed her quickly faded. As I sat waiting, she turned her head over her shoulder:

— You can have one of those fags if you want.

I should have said no; I hadn't smoked in years, or certainly not sober. But perhaps there was still a little alcohol in my bloodstream because I did want one. The packet said Smooth. That sounded good.

By the time she'd come back to sit with me, I'd fished one from the pack. She pushed her lighter over but I couldn't coax a flame from it. I shook the thing and tried again. Scratched on the lighter's back was what I took at first to be a rune – but no, I realised, it was a crude head and shoulders, poking in through an odd wide window. Was it?

Angie plucked the thing from my fingers, and with a simple flick of her thumb, lit my cigarette.

Not a quarter-way through, I realised my mistake and stubbed it dead.

— Sorry, said Ange. — Shouldn't have tempted you, should I?

— I'm a big boy. If I didn't want one, then…

She looked at me, as though calculating something.

— You do know your own mind, do you?

I thought then, that she was in some way flirting with me. No. I was sure of it.

I realised also that I had been wrong. She was much younger than I had thought: younger, but somehow used up.

— I don't know how you can stand it, she said.

When I asked what, she smiled:

— Riding round. With him.

— It's just business.

The kettle clicked. She got up and busied herself at the side.

— It's the people, said Ange. — That's what I don't like. Too many fucking crazies.

She was talking about the charity shop workers, wasn't she? And hadn't Harris tried to convince me of exactly the same the night before? I felt a vague suspicion start to ache at me.

— Most of them are just old dears, I said. — A little bit lonely, mostly.

— Some of them are. But some of them are also –

She threw her hands in the air. I didn't know really what to say. But Ange hadn't finished:

— Well, we all need to get out of the house... Don't we?

I had the distinct impression that she was accusing me of something. She came back to the table with a mug of tea. I took a draft: a mistake. It had a faintly greasy aftertaste of peppermint, as if mixed with the run-off or slurry from a deep-fried After-Eight. And when I looked at the liquid's surface, sure enough I could make out a couple small pools of oily iridescence.

— All sorts of people get exploited, she said.

She seemed to be watching me closely, waiting for a reaction, as though there was something profound in what she'd said. Or some hidden meaning. Then again, perhaps she was waiting to see if I'd have more of her disgusting tea. I almost did, just to be polite, but my stomach lurched and, quite reflexively, I thrust the mug away. Angie looked rather put-out.

— So... How do you know Harris? I asked: a weak attempt at distraction.

— I don't know him.

She had taken offence again. Again, I had said something wrong. But Harris *had* made it quite clear that he was on favourable terms with the owner of the lodgings. That was her, wasn't it? I scrambled for something to say, however inane.

— Do you think he's one of the crazies?

She looked at me with the disdain the question deserved. Yet after a moment something seemed to occur to her.

— Well, she said. — I don't suppose I'll see you again, now. She smiled: the good smile again, the one that had worked so well on me earlier. — If you drink your tea, you might just get pudding.

Pudding – after breakfast? I really didn't get it – neither did I want it, whatever it was.

— I'm sorry, I said. — It's just that nothing's sitting right on me this morning...

It was roughly true.

But Angie was already up. She crossed back to the sink. I caught a glimpse of her reflection, her face flat and distant in a small section of shaded window. Outside the wasps continued to dive-bomb the glass.

I waited an hour: nothing from Harris. I'd already called his mobile a number of times, the thought of the huge unwieldy handset – with its glowing green screen and translucent white plastic keys – enough to see me chuckling to myself. Each time it just went through to voicemail. I had noticed the night before that coverage had been patchy around the town. And despite Ange living locally, and having spoken with Harris before he left, she didn't have any specific idea of where he might be.

About twelve forty-five, I called him again. This time my

call was answered – but only by the sound of breathing and then a sigh of exasperation. But then:

— Why doesn't it work?

It was Harris's voice, all right, followed by the click of disconnection and the moaning monotone of a dead line. Two more attempts and finally Harris got it together enough to speak to me. And that was about as far as he got. He was mostly incoherent; I had to assume that he was either drunk or high on something. Eventually I had it from him that he was in an arcade of some sort; that tallied with the semi-musical pips and beepings I could hear in the background, along with the breezy light sound of children – the rustle of high-pitched murmuring breaking into occasional shrieks of excitement or joy. Disconcertingly, for just a second my imagination spasmed; the voices I heard, I was certain, spoke in a tongue alien, if not wholly unfamiliar. I could almost see the place: brightly lit signage and vending stations, pictograms, like movieland sci-fi, or –

— You need to come, Harris said.

Then some young, gleeful voice near the receiver at the far end cried out a suggestion definitely Anglo-Saxon in origin, and that mental image of mine was lost, burst like a firework.

I told Harris to stay where he was, that I'd find him.

He seemed to agree, but I had no faith that he'd actually understood me – or would remember what we'd said. Of course, the fact of his being in an arcade wasn't enough information. Ange's face sank when I explained and asked her where it might be; in a seaside town, there would always be more than one.

— I thought he was in one of his moods this morning. I never should have let him go off. She shook her head. — Well, he gets his own way, doesn't he? One way or another. Even if the cost is a heart att–

Then suddenly, she was whispering, frantic:

— *That* should have been my wish. She bit down visibly on her bottom lip. — Maybe a stroke. Does he even possess such a thing as a hear-

I sighed, interrupting before the whole situation got too uncomfortable – there was clearly history between the two of them. The kind of sticky entanglement I didn't really care to imagine. Harris, I explained, more to have something to say than out of any real hope, had been jammering on about the sea, and the beach – and then, rather discomfitingly, the forest.

At that, Angie snapped her fingers. The huge arcade on the front, she told me, was quite literally called the Fantasy Forest. Our Eureka moment. The actual exclamation I made was rather less polite, and was repeated moments later on discovering that I was no longer in possession of the keys to Harris's van. He had to have taken them back that morning while I was sleeping. I shuddered at the thought of his silvery fingers passing greasily through my clothing. Yet the van itself was still parked outside. I shrugged, and reconciled myself to walking.

— You don't have to go after him.

Her tone of voice was level – to the point of affectless even. I knew full well that I didn't *have* to do anything, but nonetheless I assured her that I did.

— It's not safe, she said. And I couldn't then tell whether she was worried for herself or for me.

Even now, I don't know.

As I opened the front door, I heard Angie sniff. When I looked, sure enough, she had a tissue clutched to her nose. I can't say exactly that she was crying, but there was certainly something the matter. I asked if she was all right, and she laughed bitterly.

— You don't want to work for him. In his mind there's no such thing. Give, take, it all boils down the same. Child, parent. It's all just words. Words, human folly, patterns. He can imitate. He can't *mean*. He just *does*.

— Right, I said. — A man of action, is he?

It wasn't exactly what I'd meant. I'd meant to clarify. Yet somehow the sarcasm *was* what I'd meant. My pride had been piqued.

Angie was looking at me as though I were an idiot.

— He doesn't ever say anything. You've not realised, have you? He's not a talker.

— That makes literally no sense, I said. — I can't shut him up most of the time.

— Watch him, she said. — If you can catch him when you don't realise what you're looking at, you might get it. She tapped her head. — If you're quick, you might see. You might catch the reverse.

— Reverse?

— The *give*. It's easier to spot when you're not looking for it. When you're drunk. When you see him back to front.

I screwed up my features, puzzled. — Like in a mirror?

Ange shook her head. — He *is* a mirror.

She touched my hand. I felt suddenly sure that she *had* been offering herself to me all along. And I had that glimpse again – of a much smoother face, hidden beneath layers of disguise, as though the wear and tear had been applied with a brush, exactly as had the makeup above it.

— I – wish I had something I could give you.

The words were out of my mouth before I really understood what I was saying. From where the urge came, I don't know.

Yet it wasn't me that did the giving. I felt something hard against the top of my thigh, something slipped into my pocket.

Angie's face was close. Close enough for me to hear her whisper:

— Has he given you the bit about favours yet? About his business? Well, a favour isn't what you think it is.

— What is it? I asked.

She laughed quietly. This time there was no bitterness. What *was* there, I couldn't say.

— It's a way of getting you close enough.

10

A thirty minute walk later, sweaty and annoyed, I'd found my way down to the front via a nearly vertical park – a series of balconies, ramps, steps and gardens cut into the cliff beneath the imposing Victorian bulk of the Grand Hotel. But after a couple circuits of the Fantasy Forest I still hadn't found Harris. Worse, Angie had warned me that there were perhaps ten or twelve other arcades along the front.

I stood dithering, wondering if I should complete a final turn around the aisles of the big arcade. In front of me were vast aquariums filled with pools of stuffed dragons and Disney-licensed soft toys, waiting doleful and patient beneath pick-a-treat crane claws. It was through the glass of one of these toy tanks that I saw the man staring at me. His gaze was so direct that I felt compelled to turn away, looking back inside to the grimy Axminster that lay incongruous beneath the sheen and gizzle of the colours of the laminated, embossed pleasure machines. He reached me perhaps a few seconds later, and wasted no time in letting me know what was on his mind:

— You try the cinema there, pal. That's where you're gonna find what you're after: your friend. Fucker's run in there.

Another glance at his face confirmed what I had already thought – I didn't know the man – or at any rate, recall him. Buzz-cut grey hair and fat, ageing features were plastered all over Scarborough, on every other man you saw. I guessed that we might perhaps have bumped into him the evening before; that he had seen Harris earlier and remembered him, and then when I appeared…

But if I hadn't recognised his face as such, there was something else in it that I did know: cold, blue-eyed anger.

— ... get the fuck out. 'Fore I call the p'lice.

I had neither the time nor the inclination to ask why he would do such a thing – or on what, if any, authority. I merely moved out onto the pavement and past him. The cinema was just fifty metres or so down the front, the other side of the little park I'd tumbled through to get there, and the sheltered benching – like the biggest bus stop I'd ever seen – that lined its lower boundary.

His tip was good. I found Harris in a screening that had recently started – a *Star Trek* movie of some stripe; the pimply youth checking tickets in the foyer knew exactly what – and who – I was talking about. Harris had, I guessed, already posed some problems. The usher took me in and even picked out Harris with his torch, slumped in the back row, the few seats around him clear of other patrons. He seemed glad to see me; at least, he muttered something to roughly that effect. He reeked of booze, although that might simply have been from the night before. Getting him out of the auditorium proved easy enough; what happened in the foyer was much stickier.

As we neared the glass doors out onto the street, Harris began to ask repeatedly where the van was; when I told him it was back at Angie's, he began to flail, trying to pull free from the arm I'd put around his shoulders.

— I'm not going out there 'til you bring it. I can't. I can't go out onto the street. Not unless we can go. Not unless we can leave straight away.

He was pushing at me quite violently by then, and I had to let go of him. That I juggled calming Harris with reassuring the by-then bug-eyed usher, whilst simultaneously wheedling the number of a taxi firm, seems now a miracle of self-possession. Yet somehow I got through to a dispatcher, who promised a car within five minutes. Just hearing that seemed to mollify the worst of Harris's physical twitchiness. Yet in its place, some other imperative began to prod at him – and out poured his bizarre, broken story:

— ... asleep on the beach. When I came awake, I could feel my face had cankered. Sore it was, red from the sun –

There were no visible traces of sunburn. His skin was, if anything, more waxy and pallid than usual. And then (although the force of the thought had surely been building all through my sweaty, flustered dash down to the front) I had the idea, hard and sudden and perfectly limpid, that this was not where I should be, not what I should be doing. I simply couldn't be responsible for Harris in this state; after all, I hardly knew the man. And God alone knew exactly what the matter with him was; some sort of an alcoholic episode – a drink-fuelled bout of minor psychosis, if that made any sense – seemed the best diagnosis I might hope for. What I was certain about though, was that I wanted the man off of my hands as quickly as possible.

— Fucking sky had come untethered. Running fucking loose. Fulcrum slipped.

A full, coherent sentence was clearly too much to ask. Moreover, despite the derangement of his story and general behaviour, when I looked at him then, he appeared quite tranquil. And although his face had lost none of its worn, detailed lines, it seemed somehow newer, as though a freshly *drawn* representation of middle-age. The distance in the gaze, his unsmiling lips – hiding those well-tartared teeth of his as they did, the smile-creases at eye-side dormant: all of this lent his face the exemplary quality of a natural, handsome actor, a screen idol, a god. It unsettled me to see such a face break, start quivering at the sight of the sky beyond the foyer, high and blue and perfect, with clouds skating in on the coastal breeze toward us. Looking out, I didn't see what could be the problem.

But another difficulty just then presented itself. The foyer attendant, stammering and blushing, came to ask us to leave. From leaning over to listen to Harris, I stood up over the poor adolescent, and let him know what I thought. The confrontation left his acne pulsing with LED intensity; that, in combination with his wavering, fearful eyes, served to make me feel an absolute bully. And as another staff member made his way over to us – this older, pudgier, more hateful man clearly the puppet master behind our ejection – Harris began singing, in the put-on voice of a small child:

> *Terry went to sea*
> *Katy brought him back*
> *Frankie came to me*
> *Fingertips gone black*
>
> *Elsa ate the sky*
> *Then she put it back*
> *Sooky's asking why*
> *I put her in the sack*
>
> *Licia smiles at me*
> *Knows she can't go back*
> *All the way back home*
> *Fallen down a crack*

Both men retreated from us, repulsed.
And then the taxi was outside.

I had to lift Harris and carry him out to the car. It was out on the front, one foot on the pavement, one in the car, that I caught a hurried glimpse of the thing that had frightened Harris so. It was a vision that opened over at the Fantasy Forest, where my eyes mis-happened upon the crew-cut man who had earlier approached me. He stood outside and seemed to be whispering to a tall, green plastic crocodile, or perhaps dragon, with a huge, toothy grin – part of some kiddie's amusement.

And after that bizarreness, at a flash, I suddenly *saw*.

Everywhere I looked I found them: flat, jagged forms, green and tall and featureless. They were thin, depthless – and their slow-fast movement bewildered me at a fundamental level, moving indifferent to the particulars of space and time and gravity as my mind understood them. A yawning vertigo enveloped me, my balance shot. I practically dropped Harris to the pavement. Somehow I had the sense to reach out my hand to the roof of the taxi. That steadied me. And by then Harris had recovered sufficiently to power himself the remaining half yard to the vehicle door. He took an age to get in; all that time I was forcing myself to focus on the hard immediate fact of the car and its sturdy, reliable frame, afraid to look up, to let in once more that gaping dizziness.

Finally I was inside, the door shut.

I didn't look out of the window, attending instead to Harris. That way I wouldn't have to think about how I was feeling; that way I wouldn't have to think about those shapes. It was a technique I had learned in my late teens, when I had done things I wouldn't do anymore, a means of getting through trips that threatened to turn sour: focusing energy on helping someone else.

— Sunstroke, the driver tried to tell me. — That's what

82

your friend has.

Was that what I had experienced as well? I told the man to shut the fuck up.

11

My next problem, after getting back to Angie's, was finding the keys to the van. All I could get from Harris was that he didn't have them with him. The first thing I did was to go up to our attic room and gather our belongings. Harris had brought only a small leather knapsack with him. I hesitated a moment before looking inside, perhaps fearful that I might find something I'd rather not see. But the keys weren't in there and the knapsack was almost empty. Inside was a single garment – underwear or undershirt – of yellowed cotton, a rusted tobacco tin, which I couldn't open, and a roll of bandaging. Nothing else.

When we'd arrived back, I'd called out Angie's name, without response. On the way back downstairs from the attic, I knocked at the door from behind which I remembered her appearing the night before. There was no answer, and I entered anyway.

Inside, it was clean and bright: filled with sun. The white-painted walls and floorboards made it so sparse and bright that I doubted briefly it could be anyone's room. But then I saw the traces of homeliness – the frilled edge of the bedstead, the shoes lined up along the radiator, a set of dark clothes laid out on the cushioned window-seat. Somewhere, up at the glass, a fly or other large insect buzzed, butting against the pane.

And there, on the far bedside table, next to a cup of water and an ashtray containing a pair of crushed, lipsticked butts, were the keys to the LDV. It was only once I had them in my hand and was turning to leave the room that I paid any attention to the wicker chair in the corner. Bulging out from its seat was what had to be the largest wasp nest I'd ever seen. It was swollen and bulbous, coloured the exact shade of weak, milky tea that the leaves of cheap paperbacks acquired after a few years. There was an odd irregularity to its shape, and I wondered if it might not be something else altogether. Despite though, those flipper-like protrusions – which might almost have been limbs and a head – I could hear a low drone coming off the thing.

The sight of it repulsed me. And I felt compelled – although not for any clear or logical reason – to destroy it. The far side of the bed there was a second chair draped with a towelling bathrobe, the folds of which seemed to be smiling at me. I wiped the robe to the floor and hefted the seat. The flimsiness of the chair made it less than ideal but I couldn't bear to use anything that would bring me into closer contact with the nest. And it was then that the image of Lyle's horrible doll – and that other queasy, half-formed assumption, which I'd pushed away at the time: that he intended for the figure some sort of wretched congress – came sharp and irresistible to the front of my mind. I shuddered at the thought. And then I hurled the chair.

The thing burst open easily; nests are only paper, after all. I turned straight away and fled the room. I had no intention of being stung for my trouble. The question of whose room it was – the why and how of the nest being in there – didn't register at all at that point.

I was on the stairs before I managed to process what I'd glimpsed in the ruins of the papier-mâché. It had been the contours of a lithe, clean line: the suggestion of shoulders and nape, flowing into a beautifully inked image of a face. An illustration – an undigested section of paper. I hadn't seen the

Mallory, I realised – the book I'd been conned into buying from Anna. Not that day – not earlier, when I'd searched my bag for the keys, or just now, when I'd looked again. I had, though, no intention of going back to examine the crushed nest. There hadn't been any of the swarm I had expected but that awful droning had intensified. But then, hadn't it given out at the end – tailed off into something like a sigh – a final, relieved expiration?

No. It didn't matter. I had the keys. We were going to leave. I wanted clear of any responsibility for Harris as soon as possible.

Back downstairs in the kitchen, I found the back door wide open – Harris was still slumped in the living room, where I'd left him. I looked outside, thinking that I might see Angie, but there wasn't anyone in sight. Something out there though, caught my eye: the pale shapes – the children's playset – I'd noticed earlier on. I didn't stop to make sure, but my impression was that they had somehow moved closer to the house. Certainly they were out now in the sunlight – it was their brightness that had attracted my attention – but that might simply have been the difference in the time of day.

12

Getting to the van was like marshalling a recalcitrant toddler. Harris, of his own volition, managed only a few steps beyond the front door before pausing to look wistfully up at the boarding house. At the time I thought him – somewhat oddly, I'll admit – regretful at not being able to say goodbye to Ange. Later – much later – I'd think differently. Very differently. Then though, I didn't waste any time in being gentle with him. I manhandled him into the van, not caring if I accidentally placed an elbow in his ribs or jaw. I think I might have managed both.

The drive back was miserable. All the way down past Sheffield, he sat peering out the windscreen through the bars of his fingers.

— It's all my fault, he said. — I shouldn't have done it. Not so soon. Not so soon. I shouldn't have done...

I told him to shut up. Moments after, I caught the edges of a schoolboyish smile barely visible behind the hands hiding the greater part of his face, an expression that rendered him all the more pathetic. Eventually though, those hands dropped and his twitchiness settled away. And yet, as London approached, I began to feel markedly worse. The dirty, guilty edges of my hangover returned and clung, fraying, at my thoughts. The *fear*. What connoisseur of the morning after didn't know it? I had the distinct sense of posing balanced at the top of a precipitous slope, at the bottom of which was Harris, abandoned and unloved, no one responding to his hideous inebriated cries for help. The thought pushed me to drive faster; perhaps too fast.

Once we had reached the spread of the capital's north fringe, I began to talk – and with a glib rapidity that felt utterly unnatural. But I couldn't bear to stay locked up within myself. So I pressed Harris about delivering my share of the stock.

He was still only able to half-mutter, half-groan his answers, but the fact that he was still apparently in some sort of pain left me hopeful that I'd be able to hash out a good bargain when it came to divvying up our load. I plotted a course straight through central London and on down to my flat. We were crossing the river before he realised, and even then he didn't object. Perhaps it was what he had intended all along.

The late afternoon sun was dreadful: stiff, still and hot. It should have been a relief to get out of the van, but it wasn't. The thought of lugging my share of the books up to the flat was just as oppressive; it smeared my already bad mood with even more foulness. Harris vanished into the bathroom for a long five minutes when we arrived. Whatever he did in there went some way to restoring him. He was at least back to making sense, but along with his recovery, his superciliousness had returned. Inevitably then, our inspection of the book load in the rear veered into disagreement.

The terrible golden clarity of the sun had performed an odd reverse alchemy on our treasure. As I looked over the contents of the first few boxes I'd unloaded, my eyes – already fatigued from the miles of brightened, glaring motorway – came close to tears. I *could* take my pick: that had been our agreement, after all, but it seemed that every book I might feasibly turn a profit on, was in some way defaced or spoiled.

Riffling the pages, I'd discovered that almost all of the good books had been in some way annotated, many extensively, whether through notes on the text itself or other scrawled information: shopping lists and bizarre prose fragments and impromptu collections of addresses and phone numbers, all jotted down wherever white space availed. Worse, the majority were also stained, or battered, or coverless. I could count on my fingers the collection I'd scraped together that passed muster: one or two merely lightly worn, with the names of their owners inked unobtrusively at the front of the book, others containing only brief, ignorable scrawls on their end pages or along their margins.

There was other stock, and much of it unmarked – but it consisted of the usual junk: failed novels by names that signified nothing to me, long-superseded editions of academic or technical textbooks and of course, crates of bestsellers that no longer sold. I kicked the boxful nearest me.

— I didn't take you all that way to increase my holdings in Clive fucking Cussler and Danielle Steele.

My voice sounded awful: childish and petulant. But there was nothing I felt able to do about it. I was swept up by a terrible guilt that I didn't fully understand. Perhaps it was that I'd let myself be swindled – that I'd been complicit in the whole con...

I looked into the van. There, dominating the interior, towered the stack of cling-wrapped books we'd taken from the recycling centre. The plastic looked shiny and pristine, especially set off against the rest of the junky crates and boxes.

— We'll break down the pallet, I told him. — I want to see what's in there.

— Nothing but crap.

Our eyes met.

— I promise you, he said.

More horseshit. I wasn't in the mood to pay it any mind.

I'd already seen the box cutter he kept in the van. Its chunky yellow handle fitted pleasingly into my hand. And slicing through the snug, staticky plastic wrapped around the books seemed simple enough.

— Don't cut into any of them... Harris warned.

I laughed – and told him that I'd be careful not cut into any of *mine*. Or did he perhaps want to do the hard work?

The very fact of the conversation proved enough to distract me; I contrived somehow to run the blade down into the tip of my left thumb. My thumbnail stopped it but the angle was such that I'd gone a good centimetre into the flesh. It hadn't hurt greatly, but blood was already welling, threatening to start slopping free. Harris understood exactly what had happened, and dispatched advice with calm disinterest:

— Press the two sides together. Keep holding it.

From somewhere in the cab he conjured a tin of plasters, flipping the lid open with weary nonchalance.

— I knew there'd be blood, he said. — Knew it. Since I woke this morning.

His fix was an expert one, even with his hands still shaking: a butterfly plaster wrapped tightly around my thumb. But before letting go he tugged at the digit.

— Does it sting? he asked.

A flurry of associations passed through my mind.

— I had a book, I told him. — One I picked up along the way. Mallory. Beardsley plates. Worth something, I think. It cost me something, at least. I don't suppose you know about it?

I caught something of the afternoon's frailty in his face then – his panic along the Scarborough front, the sadness leaving Angie's. Then he hid it. He hid it behind a look of pure, venomous spite. I hadn't seen anything like it from him before, except...

— *She* was a favourite, he said.

His words after that were caught up in a kind of roar, as though we had been immersed beneath an immense cataract. It seems stranger now, thinking back through it, than it ever seemed at the time. Then, it felt like it did to pretend the echoing of one's own blood flow in a seashell was the sound of a raging ocean, or like the lurching encroachment of a good chemical high on one's sensory experience. Perhaps I imagined that I was tuning him out: he wasn't giving me the answer I thought I needed to hear, and I cared nothing about his professed attachment to the lonely old woman at the boarding house. Now I'm not so sure. I'm not sure that I didn't hear – and understand – exactly what he said. I'm not sure that there isn't something – and a something *not* of the past – which blocks me: try as I might, I can't dig out from memory his words.

I do remember turning to look at him, unbelieving that after everything, after tracking him down in his sorry state, that he wouldn't just shut up and at least try to give me what I wanted.

By then Harris was talking once more in that hushed, scared voice of his:

— ... is what things are really like. Full of keen, dangerous edges, poised always to cut through...

I thought I had him then. He was vulnerable, and I imagined I had the chance to get whatever I needed from him.

I started soft: yet another mistake.

— Is there anything you need? I asked.

Harris shook his head.

— There's something I *want* though. Some*one*.

His eyes found mine. I don't remember him saying anything else. But I knew exactly what he was talking about: the only thing that he'd ever really wanted from me: Karen.

— She's not for sale.

His gaze stayed fixed at mine.

— You misunderstand. I think you *mis*understand.

— What, I asked. — What?

— Maybe, he said, dragging it out... — Maybe *she* already made the sale.

— Sold herself?

Harris's beard twitched. — Sold you.

I think that if he'd laughed then I would have lost it. Truly lost it.

Instead I told him that I just wanted our deal done, and my share of the books. I didn't give a shit about anything else, any of his spooky hoo-hoo or his cunty dry humour. I punctuated each of my demands with a fist to the side panel of the van.

It worked.

Harris was cowed; his recovery was clearly more delicate than it had seemed. Immediately – and despite myself – I felt guilty. I almost apologised. Almost. Somehow I managed not to. Instead, I told him to start unstacking the pallet. And when he began to cut through the plastic wrap, I felt almost happy. For a few seconds, at least.

But he had been telling the truth. The stock hidden away under the plastic was signally worthless – book club hardbacks and promo copies given away gratis with *The Times*, computer manuals for 1987 Amstrads, decade-old university prospectuses and Habitat catalogues marked with coffee-mug rings. As with the rest, the few saleable books were all compromised in some way – torn covers, extensive biro doodling, or stained and discoloured paper stock.

I'd been had – taken in by him, just the way he took everybody in: the workers in the shops, the hotel barman, Ange – everyone. I flung the water-damaged copy of Ibsen's *Ghosts* in my hand into the gutter. Harris, to my surprise, stooped down and picked it up.

— Listen, he said, stroking through the pages as though the book was a fond pet, — *you* may not want these...

That was enough. I grabbed him by the throat and pinned him back against the side of the van.

The sight of the Bricklayer's Arms, just down the hill a way, poked loose a recollection.

— Still think I look fucking dangerous? I asked.

13

The money that Harris gave me was the fan of tenners – or what was left of them – that I'd seen him take from the barman at the hotel. There was a little over two hundred pounds. He let the notes drop just before I took them from him, as if they were in some way contaminated. Given my bandaged thumb, I might have fluffed the take. But I didn't. A solitary note escaped. It eschewed delicacy, any fluttering or pirouetting. It plummeted like a hell-bound sinner.

And I was supposed to scramble after it. I left it kerbside.

Harris's little trick wasn't going to spoil the fact of victory over him – even if that success was only in being paid for all my hard grunt.

The other part of our deal was just as simple: I'd drive him back to Gunnersbury and in addition to the money he'd sort me out a box of treasures – a first edition or two, he said – culled from his special collection. He'd promised to show me the books first, but that didn't really matter. I had his money already, and so I agreed to it more out of pity, some miscalculated desire to walk away from the ruins of the weekend with at least a clear conscience. At least, so I thought at the time.

His digs were, I'll admit, something of a disappointment. Technically I suppose, the house could have been called a lodge, or even a cottage. But those terms imply a kind of pastoral notably absent from the scene. It stood on its own in a dead-end, the roadside corner of a small pocket park, half-buried in an avalanche of privet hedge. It was a modern or modern-*ish* house with tall windows, lined with dreary, ashen nets. All evidence suggested it had been built as a groundskeeper's lodgings, a place done on the cheap and long since sold off. Pebbledash cladding and the rickety, paint-peeled conservatory competed for ugliest feature. At least it had its own drive, or more accurately, a van-shaped space in the overgrown buddleia, a bush which in turn impeded the access to a rickety wooden sidebuilding, either garage or lean-to.

Grey linoleum, flecked maroon-and-white, lined the hall floor, or that small part of it visible past all the junk. I dumped a box of books from the van, a token conciliatory gesture, inside the front door. The violence of its impact pleased me: the brutal slap, the whirling motes caught in the afternoon sunlight. And the aftershock. Not an echo, but a responsive disturbance.

A susurration.

A rustling, unsettled and curious.

— Only one thing for it...

The dirty, broken reed of Harris's voice spoke from somewhere beyond the stacked boxes. He was waiting for me to speak, to ask. I knew it – and I fed him anyway:

— What?

I heard a noise somewhere between snort, sneeze and laughter. The porch was rife with a vaguely ash-like dust. It would have been nice if it had put me in mind of bakeries. It didn't. I thought instead of crematoria.

— A sour, said Harris, — made with Suntory whisky, and filled with ice. Cold, long bitch like that will fix up anything...

Somehow I'd known – or feared – that he would offer me a drink. I wanted it but demurred, glancing at the dark, unruly ranks of furniture crowding in. I demurred, but I ended up, nonetheless, with a glass in my hand: exactly how doesn't now matter. I suppose it happened for the same reason that I'd agreed to bring him and the books back to his house: it was what he wanted.

After all, when hadn't he got his way?

I remembered his little drunken speech about favours. As well as accruing them, he was expert in forcing them on others. But then, perhaps the two things were one and the same. Hadn't Angie said something similar?

At the end of the hall was a room in which Harris had summoned a gathering of chairs, like a dusty little druid circle. I sat down, but almost immediately, Harris disappeared. He'd muttered, in some typically odd diction, about preparing something. To eat, I understood.

Perhaps it was the mild discomfort of my sunburned neck, or the chair itself, low and lumpy, permeated with dust. Perhaps it was my curiosity, or even some vague avarice, but I got to my feet and wandered back along the hall. The crap shovelled in there – the shelves, the out-of-place dresser, the crowding boxes and man-high book stacks – blocked and baffled the outside light at every turn.

I realised then that I hadn't yet seen a single shelf or any other organized storage system. How could he ever locate the books he needed for his business? There had to be a stockroom or library somewhere. Perhaps upstairs. Down here there was only mess. Yet still somehow the golden early evening sun found its way through the maze of junk, gleaming from the ranks of dark wood.

— My books... I called.

There was no answer. At least, not at first. It occurred to me – and not suddenly, either: I had in truth been entertaining in a vague way the possibility, ever since getting to my feet – that I might simply leave. Walk out of the door and go. I had his money, after all.

My money. It was *my* money.

96

Yet when I looked at the fluted glass of the porch windows, I could make out someone – something – moving outside. Yet the flat, oblique movement – I can describe it no better – made me suddenly, brutally certain that, were I to open the door, I'd see gathered outside those horrible flat shapes that had glided quietly at us across the Scarborough front.

As I stood there, my heart overeager and lolloping as though played by an appallingly inept drummer, I heard the voices: low and controlled, and muffled by the adjacent walls. One of them belonged to Harris. Of that I was sure. The matter less certain was from where precisely the voices came.

I glanced into each of the other downstairs rooms in turn; I was only just beginning to appreciate just how large the house was. All of the living space though, was given over to the haphazard storage of Harris's collected junk. Finally I opened the last of the downstairs doors. For just a moment it seemed as though I'd opened a portal onto some vast workshop or crude, unindustrialised factory, the hum and rustle of lowered voices swarming. But it was only the sound through an open window of the van's gearbox as Harris attempted reverse.

The room itself was surprisingly spacious – the far wall part-removed, and opening onto the structure I had glimpsed through the buddleia from outside. I had been half-right: it was a garage, inexpertly converted to an extra workroom. Boxes of envelopes and great rolls of brown paper and bubble wrap were piled haphazardly in amongst the ubiquitous citrus fruit pallets. And then beyond that a maze of more chaos – an antique (in the roughest sense) writing bureau, overflowing with string and tape and pens. The rear of a small alabaster statue, a nymph or cherubim, its head hung with sacking. Cheap plastic stacking crates, their translucent sides showing step-towers of books.

And then I saw something that seized my attention.

An immense, mess-covered tabletop.

It took me a moment to understand that I was seeing the thing in a mirror. It was crowded with craft knives and rulers, bottles of solvent and glue, cloths and sponges and a variety of tools I didn't recognise: things that might have been used to work or punch holes in leather; an object like a hinged guillotine, its long blade shiny with grease; there were hand tools, steel and chrome both, of a vaguely insectoid character – and the longer I looked, the more organic seemed their forms. And then my understanding of what I was seeing swung altogether left of the straight.

I noticed, set up above the worktable, something that could only be a large Anglepoise lamp. Yet pouring down from it was not illumination, or light of any kind. No – it was purest dark, radiating, I suppose, from a bulb that I couldn't see. The effect was that, although I could make out most of the massed paraphernalia, especially towards the edges of the table, whatever was at the very centre, beneath the lamp, was utterly obscure.

When I tore my eyes from the mirror, I couldn't locate the desk anywhere within the room. That wasn't exactly a surprise, given the haphazard, maze-like arrangement of storage boxes and units. The table though, had appeared so large in reflection –

I moved further inside. It had to be in the garage section, hidden by the rats' nest organization, the mirror set at some bizarre angle. Was it a surprise that even the walls weren't flat? Before I could make sense of the warped geometry though, something banged against the wall. Except it wasn't a wall. It was the wide wooden door of the converted garage.

I froze. Something was outside. It butted stupidly at the door. A dog, I thought wildly. A dog wandered in from the park, off its leash. The wood planks of the door rattled, vague but insistent. And in the gap between the bottom of the door and the poured concrete floor, I could see -

— Did you need a freshener? Harris stood behind me just inside the doorway. — For your glass?

He had a small stack of books in the crook of one arm, on top of which balanced an ornate black glass carafe.

— It's all for you, he said, and it took me a moment to understand that he meant the books rather than the drink.

— Come – come, now.

— There's something... I started, gesturing at the garage door.

— Insects, he said. — The bluebottles swell right up at this time of year. And then the birds come after them – after them and the butterflies in the buddleia.

He shook his head. It was an annoyance, the gesture meant, but nothing more.

Reluctantly, and not a little puzzled, I let him lead me from the room. We returned to the odd little circle of chairs. Harris ghosted his way over to the back wall, which was really just a set of French windows covered by rattan blinds. A great crackle, followed by a small-scale boom, and he magicked some dusky, mournful jazz from a wonderfully antique sideboard with built-in speakers and a glowing, golden control panel.

— Sit, he urged. — Sit, sit.

He replenished my glass from the carafe before raising his own. Then he cracked his drink hard against mine. Liquid leapt out, soaking the plaster on my thumb and sending a sharp pain through the cut beneath it.

— These are your books.

I took the proffered stack: a hardcover on Spanish guitar construction; a tatty little paperback number on the likely military costumes of the Punic wars that he assured me was both popular and valuable, even in its middling condition; a vast world history of lace, too heavy, almost, for my lap; an immaculate but jacketless Edward Said treatise. One of the promised first editions turned out to be *The Satanic Verses* (— I wouldn't flash that around too much between here and Hounslow, Harris quipped, with his usual stale facsimile of wit, the line too practised, too old). There were others, all attractive, all somehow flawed. What more had I expected?

The last book, a hardback, was jacketless. Its boards were covered with rough sacking, and there was no wording, no author or title on the spine. I lifted it but as I did so, it slipped. It was heavier than it appeared. Somehow though, the plaster on my thumb had caught on the book. And, having been sodden by Harris's spilled drink, the bandage slipped from my digit. Without meaning to, I smeared blood over the deckled page edges.

— Oh, said Harris. There was a moment's uneasy silence. Then:

— Let me. I'll find you a different one.

And before I could think otherwise, he'd got the book away from me.

— It doesn't matter, I said.

— No, said Harris. — A mark like that – it'll change things. Transform the value. Completely...

I'd had enough of it all.

— It doesn't matter, I said again.

I clenched my cut thumb within my fist. It wasn't bleeding freely now. With my good hand, I began to gather the other books.

— How can you afford to give all these away? I asked.

— Perhaps the books are yours. Perhaps *all* the books are for you.

Whatever it was that served to manufacture his smile, it burrowed once more, forlornly this time, through his beard.

— Perhaps they were *always* all for you.

The drink had clearly gone some way to reinvigorating his bullshit generator. I, for my part, felt abysmal. The Suntory – if that was indeed what it was – had proved sufficient only to recharge my hangover, rather than burst through the other side of it.

— Haven't you figured it out yet? Harris asked. He looked almost sorrowful. — They aren't what are important. Didn't I already tell you?

I shouldn't have cared, but Harris's disappointment slew me: the perfect cap to an awful day. When had my skin become so permeable? I slumped back and closed my eyes.

When I opened them again, Harris was leaning in towards me. I could see now, at the corners of his mouth, caught in the neatly trimmed whiskers of his beard and moustache, little white deposits of scum. And I thought of Lyle, chewing away sloppily at his precious pieces of junk paper.

I felt Harris place, very gently, something in my lap.

I looked down at a vaguely familiar shape, about the size of a house cat.

And just like a cat it lay curled up, pallid and rumpled. I imagined that through the papery shell, I could make out a small, slowly pulsing shape, a twisted little figure of eight, smeared with a dark, copperish stain.

Harris's favour. Or one of his children.

Were they not one and the same?

Where he had conjured up the thing from, I don't know.

But it had, I think, been there all along. Only I hadn't seen it. I hadn't noticed it.

I hadn't *thought* it.

It didn't surprise me, though – not really. It felt like I had known about it forever.

Somehow I had the presence of mind to check Harris's fingers. There was nothing there that might have been a fresh bandage or plaster. Yet for some reason that absence disquieted me all the more.

I remembered then his saying, in some other context (I have the notion that at the time I thought he spoke of his fingers and conjuring tricks):

— They're not quick. They don't have to be. They only have to be quick *enough*.

And even though it was there, resting in my lap, and it repulsed, still I could not imagine myself touching it. Lifting it and sending it away from me.

I seized Harris's shoulder.

— What *is* it?

His face was eager. Perhaps even joyous.

— What *should* it be? he asked. — It can take you anywhere. To any dream.

Some part of me wanted to believe; but I knew he was lying. There was nothing inside the thing, nothing there but paper, chewed up and reformed. Nothing but a hollow that he wanted me to fill. I knew it was a trap. Once sprung, you couldn't let go. It wouldn't *let* you let go.

Exactly where I found the strength to refuse, I don't know. Perhaps I had seen too much already that I wasn't supposed to: Lyle and his mannequin; those flat, streaming shapes at the Scarborough front; and the wasp nest in Angie's room – the nest that wasn't any such thing. Perhaps Harris had simply reached the limits of what he could do, of how far he could compel me; I had to take the next step of my own accord.

It was just that I wasn't yet close enough. He wanted me nearer. Sufficiently close that *it* could reach me, even if it wasn't quick.

I thought about how much I disliked him. And I realised then that I had agreed to come back with him not because I wanted the books. Or because I felt pity for him – although I did, and that was part, I suppose of why I resented him so much. No, I'd come in order to play some trick on him. To steal, or spoil something that mattered to him. To teach him a lesson. The lesson that I'd thought he was trying to teach me.

It stirred then, his favour. Something stretched and rolled beneath the surface of the paper. And all of my hatred of Harris seemed suddenly massively foolish – petty and far away.

Perhaps it was that – the thought of my own smallness – which saved me.

For in the end, all I did – all I *had* to do – was to stand up. A simple thing – perhaps the *simplest*: there was no longer any lap in which Harris's little trick might rest.

I don't remember exactly what happened to it. I'm not sure that I ever knew. The only certainty I had was that the thing was no longer on me. And it is probably a trick of recollection, perhaps even wishful thinking, but when I push at the memory, all I come away with is the vision of a folded brown newspaper – the *Seattle Post-Intelligencer*, from July 1969, its headline huge: 'Man Walks on the Moon'. Practically the only thing my father bequeathed to me before disappearing. When I was a teenager old enough to have it from my mother, I'd snatched it up, unfolding it eagerly. Hoping for I don't know what. It quite literally came apart in my hands, the paper little more than ordered dust at the worn-in folds. I was left holding fragments, small and large, still stacked together but no longer a truly coherent whole. Other parts, like leaves, danced free, lilting through the air and down to the floor.

Was that what truly happened to the child – to Harris's *thing*? I hope so. Even now, I hope so. But I don't know. At least, not for certain.

What I *do* know about is Harris.

At some point during it all, he'd fallen back from his crouched, stooping position by my change. He remained down on the floor, his face slack, his eyes open and glassy. Had I pushed him away? I felt as though I might have – I might have done so without thought. On the floor, a foot or so away from him was his glass, lying empty in a pool of clear liquid. His legs were oddly splayed.

He'd kicked the drink over. He had to have.

I remembered Angie saying that odd, off thing – about wishing for a stroke or heart attack. Had she meant that she wished for it or more loosely, that Harris himself did? I couldn't quite recall.

Or was it that –

Something flickered through my mind, a thought that was both sweet relief *and* lurching terror. But whatever it was, I couldn't keep hold of it.

There was a noise then, as though Harris was trying to speak. But when I looked at him, his face was still. Only there was a movement, wasn't there? Some sort of winged insect – like a wasp, yet paler – had landed on the gunmetal hair of his upper lip. For an awful moment I thought it would creep up into the dark cavern of his nostril. But at the last it jerked away and, pursued or pursuing, launched itself into the air. I noticed then that Harris's lower lip was torn and bloody. Had he had some sort of seizure, or attack? Had he been stung?

The cut to his mouth: he had to have struck his head. Didn't he?

I don't know how long I stood there.

There was a series of questions to answer. They fell one by one, like an exquisitely designed run of dominoes.

Should I help him? Should I call some other help? Might he recover? And if so, should I let him?

They ran on and on, those questions.

I paused a moment, looking at the stack of books he'd offered me: another question, perhaps the last.

I left them where they lay.

In the pocket of my jeans was Angie's lighter. It had remained, nestled snug against the top of my thigh, ever since she'd slipped it in.

I took it out, and looked around me.

All that wood. All that *paper*.

It would burn easily.

That was the picture the fallen dominoes had revealed: a great inferno.

I looked at the scratched emblem on the reverse of the lighter's plastic case. Suddenly it resolved itself. It wasn't a rough portrait or head at all. Rotated ninety degrees it became a doorway, or threshold, through which a sideways figure eight was in the process of exiting.

Or entering. I couldn't tell.

This time when I flicked it, the wheel didn't stick.

14

For days afterwards, I hid. I slept as best I could, which wasn't well. Not at all well. I didn't realise at first exactly how frail the experience had left me. I wouldn't last ten days before my first attempt to go back: a guilty return to the scene of the crime.

Only...

Only I couldn't find the little park. Harris had directed me there. And of course I'd left in a hurry, muddling my way through a skein of unfamiliar streets, afraid to expose myself by asking for directions, or even looking at my phone. Eventually, after a long, haunted walk, I came to a station – South Acton, I think it was. Somewhere, at least, that was nowhere, and in turn went nowhere useful. I bought a paper ticket. By the time I found the centre of town, I needed to get a night bus. So when I went back in search of Harris's house – in search of whatever was left of it – I didn't know where to start.

I'd seen nothing about it in the London papers, no reports of a blaze or fire. Carefully – I used internet cafés and the local library – I searched online, checking local forums and the like, the less formal avenues of news and gossip: nothing.

For the longest time I lived in fear of a knock at the door. A police investigation. There was never anything of the sort. Not over Harris. Not over any fire.

Not an investigation in London, at least.

What then, was there?

I was never officially contacted. The Japanese authorities dealt directly with Karen's family. And they didn't do a damn thing –

It was the family solicitors who let me know.

Karen didn't ever make it home. The date of her return flight came and went.

Eventually, after what I understood to have been a nightmarish process for her parents, the police there managed to produce her body, swept out shamefully from some dusty, under-carpet hole. The official verdict was suicide; she was found in woodland at the foot of a notorious drop. Of much of the detail I can't be sure. Her parents didn't want to speak with me; clearly, she'd vented her unhappiness to them. Even if they could have held their noses, I'm not sure that they actually had anything to offer. The translated reports were stiff and detail-free. It was only because one of her friends felt I ought to know, that I heard the rumour of an affair – an unhappy one – with an older, married colleague.

In the end, I got the flat. Her work provided repayment cover whereby in the unfortunate event etc. etc., a substantial chunk of the mortgage was paid off; the woman from HR, or their legal services division, or whatever it was, explained rather sniffily to me that despite being named as the beneficiary, I didn't qualify for the further life insurance component. Because of the nature of Karen's demise.

I was supposed, I inferred from her tone, to be upset about this – over my non-qualification for a payment about which I had, up until then, known nothing. Karen had never mentioned nominating me; or if she had, perhaps during a drunken conversation – the time when we did most of our communicating – I remembered nothing of it.

Once the reality of the situation had sunken in – and this all happened during a period of no more than five or six weeks after the awful trip North – I hit the wall. And I hit it hard.

I lost myself on a bender which, had I not experienced the visit to Scarborough with Harris, would have counted as the most terrifying, the most miserable thirty-six hours of my life. I felt convinced I was being followed. Shadowed. For the first time in my life, drunkenness was a proposition worse than sobriety. Instead of tamping down my nerves, the booze fuelled the worst of my imagination.

Being wrecked wrecked me. All the while I felt as though something followed me, padding always just out of sight.

I went home and hid.

By January I was completely dry. By Easter all my saleable stock was gone; I dumped the rest. I couldn't bear the thought of taking it to a charity shop. By summer I'd left London and put the flat on the market.

I moved to Bridgend, where a pair of old university friends, long married, had ended up. I stayed in the summer house at the bottom of their garden for a month. It was partly – mostly, I suppose – out of a sense of obligation to them that I took the job in Cardiff. Not long after that I met someone. We clicked, or almost; enough to get a place together. But I suppose I'm not the easiest, or most attentive, person with whom to share a life.

There had been a steady accumulation of differences. And other problems. We'd talked about buying somewhere. I had money, and a lot of it –from the pending sale of the flat. Sarah wanted children. I – I wasn't so sure...

I'd been having anxiety dreams. Things – everyday things – worried at me. One Friday, after dinner and a glass or two of wine that I shouldn't have had (I didn't, not anymore), I dreamt that Sarah went away on a business trip. But it wasn't *that* dream – a replay of the past. No – in this dream, Sarah came back. It should have been happy. But it wasn't. Sarah had changed. She was wrong. She wore the dead, painted eyes of a marionette. I couldn't stand to be near her. It was a relief when she left the room.

And then I heard her calling out from the bathroom, her voice like a worn cassette tape. She wanted to know where her hairbrush had gone. Quite why that frightened me so, I didn't want to remember.

Neither do I remember waking, or what I said. For her part – and for whatever reason – Sarah couldn't bring herself to tell me. I knew though that whatever had happened, she was un-happy. But instead of confronting her, I let it all slide. I had a difficult week ahead at work. That was what I told myself.

Sarah left, without saying anything, the following week-end.

The month after that, while boxing up my things in order to move on yet again, I found the book.

World War II Destroyers. I have it with me now. The name on the cover, Jacobs, is the same shade of sun-faded pink.

Finding it then annoyed rather than surprised me. I'd tak-en very little care in gathering my possessions when I left Lon-don. The book was stashed in with a number of others at the bottom of a used removal firm box that I hadn't ever prop-erly unpacked. When I found it I was looking for stuff to toss in order to make more packing space for the things I *did* want to keep.

As soon as I lifted the book, a grey caul, no larger than the palm of my hand, detached itself and went floating, like a silken leaf, to earth. I realised, with a kind of gritty unease, that it was nothing more than ash. Inside the book, tucked under the fold of the dust jacket (the *wrapper*, I reminded myself, with a shudder), was a sheet of paper.

It had been folded – of course it had! – several times initially to form a long, narrow oblong. And that oblong in turn had been folded, twisted, concertinaed – I have not the necessary technical wherewithal to describe – into something like a rectangular ring. A ring with a twist somewhere along its length. It was the work of a few seconds to deconstruct the thing.

Paper. Two sheets. A pale, watery blue. Thin. And fragile. Airmail, I thought. But by then I had seen the handwriting.

It resembled, quite remarkably, my own. I read it, and doing so, a great disquiet settled down upon me, drifting in on my shoulders, just as the ash had fallen so placidly from the book.

By then I was certain – or almost certain – that the handwriting was my own. Yet I didn't remember ever setting any such thing down on paper. And I certainly had no memory of the events described. The script itself appeared a fragment of some longer missive. The sentences at page top, and page bottom on the reverse, were incomplete.

What it told of, though, seemed to make sense – if only at a very rough level. It was a recollection – (*my* recollection?) – of a visit to Harris. Except the visit seemed to take place in a grand apartment bearing little resemblance to the house to which he'd taken me.

Here:

... something I'd been about to do, yet I couldn't remember what.

I looked around for a cue.

It shouldn't have been any surprise that there was no answer when I called out to Harris. Only my own only voice, slapped back from the echoing spaces of the vast apartment and its gleaming hardwood surfaces.

The next thing I remember is the cardboard carton. Harris, I suppose, had come and gone, thrusting it upon me. Stacks of thin, flat card filled it – paper and card. Card and paper.

"Bookmarks," his voice told me, echoing from some unseen corner of the room, brushed up with an oddly excited pride. "All of it. Everything in that box."

"You use these as bookmarks?" I asked, confused.

"No," replied his disembodied voice. "They're not that anymore."

"Then they're –" I paused, thinking hard. "Your real business – these are your real business?"

But the only answer I received to that question was the box itself: the box and its contents. I found greetings cards, ancient train tickets, hastily scrawled shopping lists, till receipts, old Post-it notes, yacht club memberships, postcards, magazine articles, torn-out personal ads and obituaries, even an expired Access credit card. A boarding-card stub, destination airport NRT, Tokyo. A pressed flower, a simple white clover.

And then the photographs, of varying sizes, stacked clumsily together and bound up with a rubber band:

A shot of a photo-board outside a French porno theatre ("Angelique Petite Fille Perverse"), the board jostling with glossy black-and-whites, blurred and dirty in the reproduction. Pictures of children, of families. And the intimate snaps: poorly framed, partly blurred, full of the dimples and scars and imperfections of human flesh – a grinning, bobbed brunette in black underwear, moles along her collar bone and stomach; an elderly gent, the Kodak paper ripped clumsily in two as though someone was missing, the man sunburnt and smiling, pinned back by the camera's flash between a table and a bleached, rustic wall. It was a snapshot from a holiday in the south of France, I felt sure, although I couldn't say quite why.

I asked their purpose: why Harris kept them. I'm sure he had *an answer*, although I can't now bring it forth in my mind. Or not exactly. But I know what it came down to: the photos, the junk – all of it retrieved from books, he'd have me believe – had an actual transferable value. A value outside of whatever meaning they might have had for the people who had taken the shots or abandoned their bookmarks. Scrawlings and annotations were what he chased – not the books themselves.

He was crazy.

I caught then, as if for the first time, his particular personal odour, delicate and dirty: uncared for. That smell, I suppose as much as anything, caused the swell of compassion – of misplaced compassion – that I felt then for him. The feeling ended when I found the strip of photos: my face and Karen's, a bookmark that belonged – or *had* belonged – to me. And I understood: it had been insert rather than book that Harris had, all along, wanted.

"What should I do with them?" he asked.

I wondered if I had spoken my thoughts aloud; for Harris had done it again, turned what was inside, out. And now he had started, he seemed unable to stop.

"Last chance," he said. I had a feeling he didn't know exactly what that meant. "That angel. That girl. She gived it up to you, didn't she? Gived it right up. She offered, yes? Made you king, did she? King bee?"

"No." The word was curt on my tongue. But it was a word that meant nothing to Harris.

"All the same, I'd like my payback," he said. "I'd like it now."

112

I was looking at him incredulously by then. I let him con-
tinue, just because I had to hear it. I had to know what he
thought he –

"Those photos," he whispered. "We agreed, didn't we? All
that long, long ago? Someone agreed. I think we agreed. I
think we did."

He had brought his chair close up to my own, and when I
looked, I saw that he was fiddling with something. I suppose
now that he wanted me to see it. But then – back then – I was
too slow. I hadn't at first recognised what it was he had. Or
at least, not recognised its significance: I saw quite clearly that
in his hands he held a hairbrush. He was trying – unsuccess-
fully – to untangle some of the long, mousy-brass hairs stuck
in amongst the bristles. What it took me longer to understand
was that I knew the brush. It belonged to Karen. Had he sto-
len it, or –

When I asked what he thought he was doing, he dumped
the brush in my lap.

"Pull out some of that hair, and give it to me."

"What is this?" I asked.

And what did I expect – an answer?! Harris wouldn't an-
swer. He didn't ever answer. He just looked back at me, his
face motionless: a trick, one of his simple tricks. He'd wait and
wait. He wanted me to be the one to speak next; I was sup-
posed, I think, to convince myself. The desire to attack, to
obliterate *him, came so close to overwhelming me that even*
now I can't be sure it didn't happen.

What I do remember is his distracting me, painting out a
memory in words: Karen talking about Saint-Exupéry's The
Little Prince. *We'd known one another then for perhaps six*
weeks. Her dogged, little-girl love of the book, I remembered,
had enchanted me. And how well she'd preserved that edition

113

from her childhood: it had been old even as she was young. But then hadn't I, Harris asked, sold that very same copy some time in the dark weeks at the fag end of winter, after Karen had flown away?

I stood up, swaying a little. And suddenly some switch, which had hung forever in the balance, fell.

"I don't want this," I told him.

I had come slowly to a realisation of something: that Harris didn't really care. His face, free from any kind of eagerness or avidity, appeared oddly slack. Whatever I did was of little real consequence – not to him, anyway.

It was like viewing an optical illusion from some slightly off angle that reveals the exact contours of its trickery. Harris – that apparent unity made up of his body, his physical presence, his voice and words – was nothing more than a lure. His moving eyes and lips and limbs differed from a painted wood puppet only by degree of complexity. I thought of his telling that there were two kinds of prop – one that was the trick itself, and one that distracted attention from the trick. Then I thought of predatory deep-sea fish and the light organ they dangle in front of their jaws to attract their prey. And I wondered what unblinking eyes were there, obscured behind Harris, weighing up the things that came swimming into the circle of illumination that he cast.

As if in answer, Harris's smile returned: teeth and shiny lips flashing out of the gloom like sequined embroidery on a train of black velvet rustling past. And if I could almost see that velutinous cloth, then also I could sense the presence that moved it – great, shadowed, queenly: too tall and too distant for the space in which we were enclosed. And then it was gone – perhaps it hadn't ever been there at all – and all that I had was the room and Harris.

Finally, I have just the fringes – the fragments *– of my egression. I cannot call it an escape.*

A glimpse of the apartment's windowless bathroom; my own uncomprehending reflection in the mirror. Harris – or someone – banging the door.

Outside in his library-like hall, dwarfed by the mahogany ceiling-high shelves, plucking books at random from the expensive, polished wood. All of them damaged, scribbled-upon, defaced with every sort of handwriting, many with pages missing, some torn out, some neatly excised as though with craft knife or scalpel.

The little occasional table between doorways, piled with letters and packaged books, Harris's missives and gifts, ready to be sent out into the world. Wrapped all in sturdy brown paper, a spiderish, scuttled hand addressing them. And the stamps, delicate little collages, mosaics of paper, paint and ink, intricate designs satirising the regent's head, too wild to be counterfeit, too precise to be anything else.

I remember tumbling the mail to the floor, stamping down my feet on the packages, the letters, the books...

And the paper...

Paper tearing like skin. Skin tearing like paper.

Words trailed after me as I strode down the impossibly long, dusty hall towards a front door that seemed to recede however hard I marched at it. I heard Harris call out one last promise in that cool, uninvested voice of his, the one he hid until you got close enough. That voice called out after me saying that the world was moving on; no, that it had already gone and that I'd spent too long with him; I'd spun away from its gravity, been left behind.

"Above you," he called out. "You'll see your sky turned yellow, the clouds glassy and thin. We'll have – arrived again. Or you'll have –"

He hadn't tried to stop me. And when I had turned to glare at him, my gaze full of anger, he'd looked back only with indifference.

I meant nothing to him.

Although I wonder exactly why *he chose to show me that? And I wonder as well why ...*

There the account ends.

I think at it, and think, and it makes no sense. I have nothing, no recall of any of the events written there. But it binds me all the same. It convinces me. Images drift, rustling into my mind: dead, imitation eyes: beads and buttons, wet pebbles.

Sigils in brown ink haunting old, brittle paper.

I think of what started my unease, of what seeded those arguments, the violent disagreements, with Sarah. Of what hounded me out of London. Of the fortnightly train trip to Bristol for my client meetings. The tunnel just this side of Newport. The pale, bloated thing clinging high and gravid at the black, water-trickled stone. The fields and copse out alongside the A48, site of the long defunct Forest Funland and its abandoned adventure playground, closed in by trees and blackberry brambles, glimpses here and there of its empty-eyed, sun-bleached fibreglass attractions.

In my worst depths, when I think I sense it again, that shadowy presence, padding just out of view, I wonder if there is anywhere I can go to escape. In my sleep, I sometimes hear Karen weeping, telling me she is sorry, sorry, so very sorry...

But it never lasts: the thoughts pass, the panic dissipates, leaving me still and calm. At times, bemused. Or perhaps simply complacent.

I know that I am all right. I *have* to be all right. Harris is dead, his papers burnt, and all because I wished it.

And after all, I've done nothing wrong.

Have I?

Acknowledgements

First of all, immense thanks and love are due to Kechi, who has made this possible in so many ways I could not begin to list them all.

Huge thanks go to my parents, Mariette Clare and Robert Bennett, for all their love and encouragement and support. Also to Richard Johnson for likewise. And finally to Richard and Margery Nzerem for continued support and child-wrangling.

Massive thanks next to Justin David and Nathan Evans for taking this on, for the nitty-gritty of book production, patience, sharp eyes, common sense and general know-how – and especially to Justin for his wonderful cover designs. Both Olivia Bays and James Greig are also due immense thanks for their sharp eyes and excellent suggestions!

There have been many people who've given me specific support, and / or feedback on various sections of this book. Thanks for this to Annie Murray, Joshua Davis, Mandy de Waal, Sophie Morgan, Jake Jones and Justin David (again!) as well as all the other talents at Leather Lane Writers. Also huge thanks are due Gul Davis and Katy Whitehead, and all the other crafty and kind members of Collier Street Writing Group, who've read and detailed their responses to my work.

There are various other individuals who have helped and encouraged and inspired me at various stages with various things, so big thanks to John Brewster, Ed and Margaret Bennett, Peter Wocha, Anthony Cartwright, Ramsey Campbell, Neil Lawrence, Phil Jell, Keme Nzerem and Kate Franklin, Richard Payne, Michael Dovey, Jason Lee, Daniel Feutz, Ben Pollock and Anthony Hossack.

Thanks also go to Djuna and Hal, who have delighted and inspired and occasionally added odd keyboard characters to my manuscripts.

And last but not least a special mention to my very dear brothers, Joshua and Nathaniel, for all their love and acceptance over the years.

Also from Inkandescent

He's Done Ever So Well For Himself
by Justin David

As a little boy, growing up in the half of the country decimated by the harsh economics of Mrs Thatcher, Jamie dreams of rubbing shoulders with the glamorous creatures from the pages of *Smash Hits* – only to discover years later that once amongst them, the real stars in his life are the ones he left behind.

Not least, his mother Gloria whose one-liners and put-downs are at as colourful as her pink furry mules and DayGlo orange dungarees. All of this, she carries off with the panache of a television landlady.

Jamie swaps the high heels and high hair of 80s Midlands for the high expectations of London at the heart of 90s Cool Britannia. He's drawn towards a new family of misfits, fuelled by drugs and sexual experimentation – from which he must ultimately untangle himself in order to fulfil his dreams. This bitingly funny tale of conflict and self-discovery is *page-turning friction*.

'For anyone who's lived and loved and fought to be the person they're meant to be'
MATT CAIN

Also from Inkandescent

AutoFellatio
by James Maker

Apart from herpes and Lulu—everything is eventually swept away

According to Wikipedia, only a few men can actually perform the act of auto-fellatio. We never discover whether James Maker – from rock bands Raymonde and RPLA – is one of them. But certainly, as a story-teller and raconteur, he is one in a million.

From Bermondsey enfant terrible to Valencian grande dame – a journey that variously stops off at Morrissey Confidant, Glam Rock Star, Dominatrix, Actor and Restoration Man – his long and winding tale is a compendium of memorable bons mots woven into a patchwork quilt of heart-warming anecdotes that make you feel like you've hit the wedding-reception jackpot by being unexpectedly seated next the groom's witty homosexual uncle.

More about the music industry than about coming out, this remix is a refreshing reminder that much of what we now think of as post-punk British rock and pop, owes much to the generation of musicians like James. The only criticism here is that – as in life – fellatio ultimately cums to an end.

'a glam-rock Naked Civil Servant in court shoes. But funnier. And tougher'
MARK SIMPSON

Also from Inkandescent

THREADS
by Nathan Evans & Justin David

If Alice landed in London not Wonderland this book might be the result. Threads is the first collection from Nathan Evans, each poem complemented by a bespoke photograph from Justin David and, like Tenniel's illustrations for Carroll, picture and word weft and warp to create an alchemic (rabbit) whole.

On one page, the image of an alien costume, hanging surreally beside a school uniform on a washing line, accompanies a poem about fleeing suburbia. On another, a poem about seeking asylum accompanies the image of another displaced alien on an urban train. Spun from heartfelt emotion and embroidered with humour, Threads will leave you aching with longing and laughter.

'In this bright and beautiful collaboration, poetry and photography join hands, creating sharp new ways to picture our lives and loves.'
NEIL BARTLETT

'Two boldly transgressive poetic voices'
MARISA CARNESKY

Also from Inkandescent

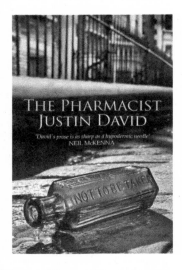

THE PHARMACIST
BY JUSTIN DAVID

Billy is just twenty-four, a young man drawn into the sphere of Albert — The Pharmacist — a compelling but damaged older man and a veteran of London's late '90s after-hours scene. A chance meeting at Columbia Road Flower Market, in the heart of the East End, leads to an unconventional friendship. As their relationship grows, driven by Albert's strange narratives and his endless supply of narcotics, the ordinary foundations of Billy's own life shift and change. Alive with the strange twilight times between day and night, consciousness and unconsciousness, this is a story of love, of loss and alienation.

"At the heart of David's The Pharmacist is an oddly touching and bizarre love story, a modern day Harold and Maude set in the drugged-up world of pre-gentrification Shoreditch. The dialogue, especially, bristles with glorious life."
JONATHAN KEMP, author of London Triptych

"An exploration of love and loss in the deathly hallows of twenty-first century London. Justin David's prose is as sharp as a hypodermic needle. Unflinching, uncomfortable but always compelling, The Pharmacist finds the true meaning of love in the most unlikely places."
NEIL McKENNA, author of Fanny and Stella.

Also from Inkandescent

FEMME FATALE
by Polly Wiseman

Nico and Valerie Solanas – Warhol's muse and would-be assassin – meet, in this black comedy about fame, failure and firearms.

The Chelsea Hotel, New York, 1968. Nico, German actress and singer with The Velvet Underground is waiting to shoot her role in Andy Warhol's latest movie and for her lover, Jim Morrison, when her room is invaded by Valerie Solanas, radical feminist and would-be Warhol assassin. A duel to the death begins...

One hundred years since women got the vote, and thirty years since Valerie and Nico died, Polly Wiseman reimagines two female pop culture icons at the epicentre of '60s cool battling for control of their own destinies.

'Wiseman's writing sears and burns.'
THE GUARDIAN

'Wiseman's challenging and sensitive play is perfectly pitched.'
THE STAGE

Sign up to our mailing list to stay informed about future releases:

www.inkandescent.co.uk

Follow us on Facebook:

@InkandescentPublishing

and on Twitter:

@InkandescentUK